John Jennings

THE MONARCH

Copyright © 2021 by John Jennings
All rights reserved
Published in 2021

Not a character in this book represents a real person
nor do any of the happenings within this work of fiction
represent anything real. Although set within the confines
of Northern England and certain parts of the island of
Ireland, all locations, although sometimes representing
actual places, have seen nothing resembling the events
portrayed within these pages.

To my wife Karen,
Thank you for listening.
Thank you for reading.
Thanks for talking.

"We must be willing to let go of the life we have planned, so as to have the life that is waiting for us."
~ E. M. Forster

Chapter 1

Sandwiches of ham and peas pudding, cheese and onion and tuna, in the form of quartered triangle sliced white bread, open buns and the odd brown sandwich from a sliced loaf were laid out making the bulk of the food, which was arranged on a large four by eight foot plyboard laid across two benches in one corner of the lounge bar. Large pork pies, beside pickled onions, beetroot and chutney, along with chicken drumsticks, both regular and tandoori, were strategically placed so anyone could reach from any side of the board. This board, once in regular use, was now placed like this in the lounge only on special days, usually those connected with Jerry's family. Today, the wedding day of Jerry's niece Linda, was a proud day for all, and nothing would spoil this long awaited occasion. No expense spared, as Jerry had proudly opined looking at the amassed food, and opening four bumper cheese and onion crisp packets, which he emptied onto a dinner plate next to the two bowls of peanuts – salted and dry roasted.

The lounge thronged with numbers seen seldom these days, and Jerry and his staff put on a spread to ensure the comfort and enjoyment of all in attendance. Martin walked over to the jukebox. Looking down, the printed paper inserts laid out the various choices; ranks and files neatly presenting the range of music essential to boost the atmosphere of any pub lounge, but particular to today's events. He inserted two pound coins and selected A7. The state-of-the-art system selected a track from the CD system in the cellar and beamed The Beatles' *A Hard day's Night* into the people sat around the seating and tables spaced regularly around the perimeter walls. Blue velveteen sofas and stools around seven round copper topped Britannia tables. Jerry had ordered the young barman to get the party started, and he then selected C8, J2, J6, A3 and finally B7.

'There's another few tracks on there if anyone wants to pick them!' he shouted at the people sat quietly around the room before looking at the two guys stood at the bar.

'Are you servin' Martin? Come on.'

'Just putting on the tracks, like Jerry said. There's some more here if you want to pick.'

'Aye Aye. Just git ower here and we'll get the drinks Man.'

'Aye. There'll be nae party till then.'

Two ladies sat in the corner, by the door, smiled and looked around.

'Its a lovely spread, mind. Though I think they could ha' had shrimps an' all. But never mind. It'll dae, I think.'

'Mind, didn't Linda look a picture. I mean, that dress. Gorgeous. You'd have thought it was made for her.'

'Well I always said Joan was the best in the toon.'

Indeed, Joan had trained and worked in London during the Sixties. People in Amble all thought of London in those days as swinging Carnaby Street, Harvey Nicks, Liberty and the small boutiques dotted on either side of the road. Never had Joan disillusioned them by mentioning the small Jewish workshop in Golders Green where she had spent three years making, altering and dispatching wedding bonnets, both diamonte and plain. Sometimes she had worked with the proprietor on the occasional luxury veil or train, but they were generally only in emergencies. When there had been a rush job. All the big work had been done by Mr and Mrs Brooks and their friend and long time assistant June.

They had all been very nice, almost maternal to the young woman, alone and lodging with friends in Finchley. But Mr Brooks, although almost in his eighties, had a wandering eye. At first she had discovered one of the pornography magazines he brought back on his business trips to Soho. Far from innocent, the twenty-two year old had looked at, marvelled at and even been excited by the images spread within the pages of the glossy magazines. Within weeks she had read, cover to cover, over a dozen of the magazines left around, sloppily secreted around the loading bay area.

It was only afterwards that Mr Brooks caught her. Up to no good, he accused, and had threatened to expose her to his wife and their assistant. Horrified, embarrassed and ashamed, she had not thought through the consequences of the exposure. If indeed he had told his wife, what would she have thought of him? What about June, their friend? No, Joan had been too shocked at Mr Brooks having caught her red-handed that she went along with him in keeping quiet about the magazines.

At first, he had cautioned her to stay quiet and await her fate. He would deal with her later. When later arrived, she had been summoned into his office after Mrs Brooks and June had left that evening. The consequences had been that Joan had left their employ, taken the bus back home to the shared flat off Finchley's Ballard's Lane, packed her bags and caught the next train from King's Cross to Alnmouth.

Nevertheless, the three years in London, far from denting

the young seamstress's reputation, had seen her working as a tailor's assistant in Alnwick. Amazing how predictions about heading off to London to make your fortune had turned out. And although she had never considered that working in George's as his assistant was in any way connected to 'making her fortune,' she was comfortably off with steady work and safe and respectable lodgings in Suzy's on Fenkle Street. There she continued to work contentedly for the next twenty-three years, in the mean-time progressing to three different addresses, the last of which now had a small mortgage left, and which, if she chose, could be paid off with ease.

George had been a good friend and boss, and before the onset of lung cancer had promoted her until she was in charge of running the place, tailoring and altering clothes as well as employing and teaching apprentices. As times progressed, and work for those around the town became harder to come by, a life line had been thrown and she had convinced her boss to go with trialling the new YOP, later YTS, staff. Everyone was happy, although some of the kids they sent weren't up to the job.

Throughout her years it had been her privilege to see Linda regularly, either in Amble or in her varied Alnwick addresses. As the years passed and the ageing lady's position and wealth slowly improved Linda began to make her way to Alnwick on her own. The X18 from Amble would drop off the girl at the bus station where Joan would inevitably meet her with ice lollies or sweets from Wilkinson's, pies and pasties from Gregg's or Dickson's, and they would walk to her home, or stroll around the town. Although people did know, there had been little fuss made of the situation. Even George hadn't made much of it and always treated her with respect. Respect, which she often felt, she didn't really deserve.

Chapter 2

Forward, the boy rocked back and forth, up and down. Shoulder height, he was 'driving Daddy' on his way up to the castle gates. This was an easy and interesting ride – watching and laughing as the gatehouse quickly grew before his eyes until he was looking up at the top of the arched gate, portcullis hanging, as about to fall – a chequered blade, ready for the drop like a guillotine.

'Look Mammy, the bricks are big,' he said as he reached and touched the smooth weathered grey stonework.

To the right, eastward, the sea stretched to the horizon, wind flecking the tips of waves. A cobble bounced slowly a mile or so away. Dark blue, white trimmed, complimenting the greyness all around, above and below, beyond the bright green grass in front.

'Get off now Son – you're getting heavy now – don't....'

The child sulkily dropped from his dad's hands onto the small tarmac pavement. His mother grabbed his hand and walked into the entrance booth to pay.

Whoosh!!

The jet swept quickly over the battlements, hedgehopping its way North and out to sea – an exercise in war. Regularly seen around here. The boy shouted after it. Laughing and jumping over the grass toward the cliff.

'Come back Aidan!' The boy's father rushed over the field, down towards the clifftop in pursuit of the 4 year old, still romping up and down and hurtling towards the edge.

'What the Hell are you doing Col?' The mother shouted before following in pursuit. All three chased the edge before coming to a halt. A group coalescing before the boom out before them in the greyness ahead.

'Look Dad. Look at the plane.'

'Aye son, its alright. Its what's called an exercise.'

'Do them with Mammy.'

'No son. It means they're practising, that's all. Not like we do in the house. It is just the pilots practising with targets. Good eh?'

'What the fuck's going on, Colin?'

'Its an exercise. Obviously.'

The family turned. The boy pointing to the plane arcing its way to the horizon beyond.

'Hang on a bit. I'll just change it'

Colin watched the blonde girl disappear through the back and turned to his wife.

'I don't know, do I?'

'But it seems like a bit of a commotion.'

His wife watched the blue beams trace the walls, sirens blaring from the road outside.

Peace then returned as Colin sat on the red leather bar stool in front of the corner bar. A school clock ticked loudly above the roaring flame. Beneath, the snake, stuffed years before, wound itself around a branch, tail trailing on the grassy tuft, encased in a bell-jar, oak plinth brown on the slate mantle.

'I don't like the serpent,' said Siobhan. 'Looking at me with them horrible eyes.' Its tongue poked out, forked and pointed.'

'A' reet Pet. Pint o' Guinness and an Eighty Shilling.'

The ale swirled into the glass as the barmaid levered the

pump. Foam frothed, stopped and frothed as she re-tugged, and slowly turned brown, clearing from the bottom up. She placed the tulip glass slowly onto the brass tray, foam spilling into the holes below.

'I'll bing your Guinness over.'

'No. Its alright. I'll wait.'

'Mam. I want crisps.' Everyone looked down, and the boy brushed his nose with his anorak sleeve.

'Aww. He's just woke up.'

'Hello. What's your name?'

'Here, he can have these.' The girl picked up a packet of Mini Cheddars, opened them and handed them down over the polished counter.

'Mind, that's a lovely little chair, Son. Have you had a good sleep?'

'Yeah, I have,' he replied. Then looking up, gabbed the orange packet.

'Say "Thank you" Aidan,' said Siobhan.

'Good lad,' rejoined her husband as the lad smiled and thanked the barmaid.

'Are you having a nice time?' the girl addressed the room, looking at the little boy sat below her in the buggy. 'Lovely day, eh, son?'

Aidan smiled up at her. Stuffing four crackers into his mouth, he replied: 'We saw the plane.'

The girl stared at him. Then looked at the parents and said she'd heard about it. From one of the regulars. 'Arthur's through there and he knows what's going on.'

'Oh, its just an exercise, ain't it? I used to come here as a kid. Planes were always hedgehopping and buzzing around. I always loved seeing them.'

'Not any more,' said the barmaid. 'That wasn't an exercise. Did you not see the police before?'

'Can I have another pint, Pet'

'Aye Arthur. Eighty Shillin' again?'

'I was just telling this lad that we never see planes around here now. You saw the plane the day, didn't you?'

Arthur leaned over the bar, perched on the stool before turning to face Siobhan and Colin. He ignored the boy in the pushchair before addressing the man standing in the gloomy bar.

'What? You saw the plane the day, then?'

Siobhan smiled uneasily as the ageing wiry man eyed her up and down, then turned back to her husband.

'Aye, we used to get loads of planes here once. But that was tw*enty* odd years ago. I haven't seen any here for a couple of weeks. And they aren't regular any more.'

'What's his name? Hallo Son. Are you enjoying them, Son?'

Aidan yawned, blinked and held the biscuits up to the man to try for himself.

'We saw the plane. It was exercising, wasn't it Dad?'

'That's very unusual.' Siobhan pointed to the snake.

'Oh aye. That was found in the cellar. What, ten years ago Arthur?'

He looked at the barmaid and then the serpent.

'Aye, found it still alive doon there during the Strike. It went for me but I managed to whack it first. Took some killin' mind.'

'Oh, you killed it?'

Siobhan's distaste was obvious as she eyed the yellow head peering out of the glass.

'Well aye. I didn't know what it was and it was going for me. Fangs bared and spitting like a cobra. I was scared, I can tell you. Naeone seems to kna what it is. Or where it came from. Some say its just a young ain.'

'Oh, but its just an adder, isn't it?' said Colin.

'Well have you got all neet?' said the barmaid.

Switching on the lights, the small bar's candle bulbs danced to life transforming the room, orange in concert with the blaze in the fireplace. The glass gleamed over the fireplace and the serpent seemed to hide around its branch, tongue disappearing in the gloom.

'Where's the snake? Where's it Mam?'

'Its still there Son. But you just have to look harder.'

Arthur handed over the note, pocketed his change and turned again to face his audience.

'Can I get yes a drink? Do you want some pop Son?'

'This is my mate's pub, you see. I've been here ... Oh, must be twenty–odd year. As you said, we used to get a lot of planes roond here in them days. But they seemed to stop, gradually mind, about the time o' the strike. The Miners' Strike. We used to have about a dozen a week. Before we knew it, nowt. Oh, they still come ower. But not much noo. Same with the helicopters. You see, Boulmer's just up the road near Alnmouth.'

'Aye, I love Alnmouth. I used to go there a lot.'

'Aye, well that has all changed noo. Nee mair o' the yellow helicopters. Seems like he place stopped sending them out aboot the same time. Back in the Eighties. I haven't seen any. And naebody else has either.'

'Noo' the planes are still coming sometimes, but not as often. And they never used to break the soond barrier. Did yes hear that?

'Yes. We heard the explosion.'

'That's the sonic boom. Niver used to dae that until just recently. People were alwi's complainin' in them days if they did. Used to break folks' windaes. But you can guarantee, a couple of times a year, that they will gan too fast these days. I kna it's off the coast, but still.'

'What about the snake?' Siobhan sipped her Guinness for the first time, gasping at how good it tasted so far away from London or Ireland.

'Oh aye. I was comin' to that. That snake, and I had him stuffed as a trophy, mind. Well he is just a bairn. Aye, I kna' he's aboot the size of a fully grown adder. But he's not an adder.'

'Oh, I heard that idiots buy pet reptiles and can't look after them. So they abandon them.'

'Aye. Throw them doon the nettie – I mean toilet. And they end up in the sea. I know that. But this isn't the case here.'

'What then?' asked Siobhan.

'That's the point. Naebody knas where it came from. Or how it got here.'

'Aye. It's an alien isn't it Arthur?' laughed the girl behind the bar. 'I'm just popping upstairs – mind the bar for a minute, will ye?'

'Listen, I know it soonds ridiculous, but loads of people have looked at it and said it shouldn't be here. The taxidermist said he'd seen nowt like it. And the guts were all discoloured. Broon instead of red, he says.'

Colin picked up Aidan and lifted him over to the glass case, more a performance to feign interest, as he listened to the man.

'Look Aidan. Look at the eyes.'

Yes, there was something different about them. But they weren't real. Replaced by the taxidermist. And the scaly skin, just like any other snake, showed no signs of anything out of the ordinary.

'Well Arthur. It just looks like a typical python or something. Lovely specimen though.' He winked at

Siobhan who took another long draught of her pint.

Amazingly good, she thought.

'Look mate. Can you see that marking on her head. See it? The little crown like mark at the back just above her nape.'

'She's a girl?'

'Oh aye. Fought like one an' all.'

Arthur laughed as Siobhan turned away, and Colin looked embarrassed, keen to defuse what may become a sexist turn in the conversation.

'I mean, c'mon. She was like a demon. Lungin' and bitin'. Never seen the like of it. And I am not jokin' when I said I was scared. Terrifying. I had to whack her three times in all. Savage.'

'Anyway. I made sure she was dead, and then I left her down there just to be sure. When I went doon again she was still lyin' there. Lifeless. Job done.'

'She would have given me ex-missus a run for her money,' he added, laughing again.

The little boy laughed along, before his mother drank up and said they'd be going now. Colin also finished up and everyone said their good-byes.

'What a wanker,' said Siobhan when she got outside.

Colin smiled in agreement as the boy threw away his yellow packet before being scolded for dropping litter.

Chapter 3

Siobhan went over to the fridge before opening the door and picking out three kippers. The family had just taken an apartment overlooking the harbour. As she stared out over the sea to the group of islands, she looked forward to a day in Holy Island. Lindisfarne, to give it its proper name, she thought.

Last night had certainly been enjoyable, if a little weird. Never had she thought the people up here, her husband's people, the grandparents of her son were strange. She had been to Newcastle dozens of times, and it really was a great city. Like Dublin, she had always found the city alive. Buzzing and full of fun. Alright, she had witnessed a few scuffles in her time - the time she and Colin had play fought in the Bigg Market on her first visit. A big bloke came over and offered to knock his block off. She smiled a the memory. And I had been winning too, she remembered. Yes, it was an interesting city alright.

Of course, she had seldom been this far up. In fact this was the furthest north than she had ever been.

She thought of the woman in the same house yesterday. Seahouses had the oldest kipper smoke-house in the world as it was here where kippers were invented. Siobhan had always been told by Colin that kippers were Northumbrian, but had always said they came from Craster, the place they had visited on the way to the castle.

Dunstanborough Castle had been interesting, but she had

been disappointed at the ruined nature of the place. This holiday was turning into a tour of old ruins. And she was getting fed up with that. Even Aidan seemed to be getting bored of it. Never mind, Colin seemed to be enjoying it. He liked to show her around his so called home.

Placing the kippers onto a plate, she then opened the door to the microwave, inserted the plate and shut the door. Seven minutes. That should be enough time. I'll check half way through, she thought. Sufficient water, she switched on the kettle and walked over to the hall to look at the information leaflets.

Alnwick, Wooler, Warkworth Castle - Not another fucking ruin, she thought. But she knew better than that. Colin said Warkworth was his favourite place. They were on the way there on the return journey. And they'd be staying in The Sun, the glorified pub opposite the castle.

As she flipped through the leaflets on the table, she opened a small booklet. She began to read the lyrics:

The Lambton Worm

One Sunday morn young Lambton went
A-fishing' in the Wear;
An' catched a fish upon he's heuk,
He thowt leuk't varry queer.
But whatt'n a kind of fish it was
Young Lambton cudden't tell.
He waddn't fash te carry'd hyem,
So he hoyed it doon a well.

Hyem, Colin had always proudly used that word, and she had found that endearing from the outset. Part of the enigma, she had always thought. He'd told her it was part of Northumbria's link to its Viking past. Seemingly, he had met someone in Ireland with 'HYEM' on a wooden plaque outside the drive. Colin couldn't resist knocking and discussing how he also used the word 'HYEM' to mean home. He said the owner, a Dane settled in Leitrim, had been impressed and welcoming.

The words, although generally coherent, and largely colloquial spellings of English, were a little difficult for the young Irish woman to fully de-cypher. But she struggled on.

> Chorus: Whisht! Lads, haad yor gobs,
> An Aa'll tell ye's aall an aaful story
> Whisht! Lads, haad yor gobs,
> An' Aa'll tell ye 'boot the worm.

> Noo Lambton felt inclined te gan
> An' fight i' foreign wars.
> he joined a troop o' Knights that cared
> For nowther woonds nor scars,
> An' off he went te Palestine
> Where queer things him befel,
> An' varry seun forgat aboot
> The queer worm i' the well.

Clearly this legend was just another reflection of the Northern past – Palestine, she noted must be a reference to the Crusades.

The microwave pinged and Siobhan panicked. She had meant to check halfway through. Never mind. On opening the door, once the steam cleared, she viewed the plate of smelly smoked fish. Ah, lovely, she thought.

Colin walked over from the bedroom door.

'Aidan's still asleep Siobhan.'

'Yeah, he slept straight through. Thank God!'

'Aye. It must be the sea air and the long walks.'

He grabbed her from behind, pulled up her vest and rubbed her breast. One hand wandered further down, across her belly button, and further. She stopped him just inside the front of her pants.

'No, she said.

'What you been doing?' he asked. 'I've been fucked. Don't seem to be able to sleep at night. Lying awake for hours. Buzzing. Can't understand it.'

'Well, what time do you call this then?'

'Oh aye. I know. Eleven o'clock. But I don't seem to sleep until well after dawn.'

'I was looking at the leaflets and I saw this. Something about the Lambton Worm. Around here, is it?'

'Well, technically speaking, its Durham, but that is part of the old Northumbrian kingdom. North of the Humber – see?'

'But they're Mackems. The mack tea and tack things oot. We Geordies say 'make' and 'take'.'

'Cos you speak 'proper-like,' she mocked, adding the 'like' so common in the North East.

Colin laughed, and grabbed her to steal a kiss. They both relaxed into it.

'Hiya Mam. Hiya Dad'

They parted and Colin picked up Aidan.

Chapter 4

Colin laughed and asked the barman for another round.

'Not me. I'm driving,' said Richie.

'What? Don't worry about that. You can stay here with us.'

'Yes Richie. Why don't you stay? We can have a laugh and a pub crawl.'

'Aye. The Hermitage has decent food on. We had a look around this morning.'

'Oh. I don't know, said his brother. 'I should really get back. Get us a half and I'll have a think. Can I have a half o' Scotch, please mate?'

The barman took the smaller glass, clicked the switch, waited then sat it on the drip tray. The black foamy liquid cleared quickly, in contrast to the pint of Guinness Siobhan was about to drink. Although both looked similar, there was no doubt that the half was inferior. Although the logo – a Cavalier - was much more interesting.

Colin paid as Siobhan racked up the balls into the plastic triangle and replaced it above the table, resting it on the table light. They had the whole bar to themselves. In no way had Warkworth survived the ravages of successive crashes – financial crises – the new name for what this village had experienced at the beginning of the Eighties.

'I remember coming here when the strike was on.' Colin addressed the three others in the room – and the barman politely withdrew.

'This place used to be a popular touristy place once. The pubs were all busy, each in their own different ways. I witnessed a steady decline throughout that year. Miners could only rely on the goodwill of their neighbours so long to stand them a few drinks. This community was decimated.'

'Decimated?' said his brother. 'If you look around you that would have been getting off lightly. It means one in ten. The hardship suffered around here is far worse than that.'

'Aye. You're right.'

Colin looked at Siobhan, took a sip of Ex and added that this place was hit as bad as Newcastle, but the Town was able to eventually recover as opportunities eventually returned, as with any large city. Not so in this village and others like it.

'I remember this bloke my dad used to talk to. A miner. We came here one morning on the bus and the scab was heading to work, less than eight months in. Sneaking to Shilbottle on the bus.'

'Shitbottle,' added Colin. 'The locals used to cross the 'T's on all the signs. No locals there now to do it any more. Can't even make a joke about the place. The whole colliery's lying abandoned, railway lines, trucks, the lot. All overgrown.'

He looked at Siobhan and picked up his glass, lifted it in her direction, in his brother's, and took a long draught of most of the beer.

'Sod it. I'll stay. What you both havin'?' Richie walked around the corner, away from the pool table area. 'Hoo, Barman?'

'We used to come here before you were born Aidan.' Siobhan smiled at Colin. He always cheered up whenever they visited the place. 'And now we're bringing you with us. That's good isn't it?'

Aidan looked up from his hands, at which he habitually stared when strapped into his pushchair or his car seat.

Chapter 5

'Howay Man. Hurry up!'
'Aye. Piss or get off the pot.'
'Shut up Man. I'm trying to make me shot here. You can play me next.'
The small group of lads, a break off from the festivities, were making the most of the wait before Linda and her new husband's arrival. The three lads were always up for a game of pool and crammed into the small panelled side-room as Tom stopped and eyed his next shot. Back and forth he paced, stooping here and crouching in anticipation of continuing his break. Three down, he eyed the thirteen ball, this and another three stripes and he was on the black. In all the years he had based himself in this little room he had never been seven-balled – the worst outcome of any game for any player. As far as he knew he was the only bloke capable of boasting such an accolade in the entire village, and Alnwick would be hard pressed to present him with an opponent able to make such a claim. He knew, as did his two younger brothers, that this was some reputation. Such was the potency of his cue, that the Queen's Head was nearly top of the league in the area.
Anyone who wanted to play had to be serious, and Tom had his cue bought especially for him by his granddad when he was in his early teens. Riley. Although a snooker cue by rights, the young man had honed this longer more precise cue with daily practice. Again and again he had

racked up the balls into the rounded black triangle usually perched on the light hanging above the table. Whether repeatedly positioning the white in the 'D' to practice his return to baulk, setting up snooker and safety shots or playing all comers, Tom, now in his twenty-fourth year, had a fearsome reputation at the table, and therefore, around Northumberland generally. Everyone who was anyone on the circuit from Throckley and Rothbury, or Wooler, and even Berwick, had heard the name of Tom Compton.

The yellow ball ricocheted squarely into the middle of the top left pocket, rattled and rumbled slowly into the innards of the green baize topped table. Quickly Tom darted to the other end of the table, winked in aim and stooped to pocket the blue striped ball into the bottom left.

'Good shot Son!' Davy repeatedly dropped the end of his cue to the floor in applause.

Tom looked over, stooping to take aim at the purple striped ball and finely cut it into the right centre.

'Oh, Man. Canny shot.'

The three lads watched as the white bounced off the bottom cushion and trickled slower and slower until it came to a halt leaving a mid-cut red into the bottom right. Bang! The balls clattered and the black revealed itself. Tom adjusted slightly without rising from the table. He aimed and, almost without thinking, slammed his cue into the white which doubled the black eight ball into the top left pocket.

'Whatever Son!'

The three young men looked at the clock above and knew it was time to leave it. For now.

Rich walked over to the wall and placed his cue in the

rack above the blue velveteen settle. Tom picked up the chalk, twisted it centrally on the end of his Riley, wiped it with his cloth, unscrewed it and zipped it into his Rexine case.

'Its not ower yet,' said Rich.

'Aye, your reet. An' I'm next. My money's doon.'

Tom grabbed Davy's cheeks in both hands and kissed his brother and rubbed his hair.

'You'll need mair money than that if you're ganna beat us the day, Davy.'

The three exited the room and entered the lounge across the corridor.

'Martin. Let's have three Bells. Doubles.'

Davy walked over to the jukebox and was pleased to see there were freebies available.

'There's a couple of songs left on there Davy,' said the barman. 'Your dad wanted is to get the party going.'

'Cheers,' returned Davy.

Looking down at the panel below he pondered as The Rolling Stones began the intro to *Gimme Shelter.*

'Canny song!' he shouted and danced and rocked, both hands not moving from the perimeter of the jukebox top. He refocused and pressed. C8. Then J12.

'Hoo! Leave some for us.'

Tom and Rich walked over and placed three glasses on the top rim of the jukebox.

'What? Depeche Mode? Kiddin' aren't you?'

Tom hated all this modern 'New Romantic crap,' as he called it. He barged his way to the centre of the jukebox to the protestation of both Davy and the younger Richie. 'It's my turn noo,' he asserted. 'Great record Martin,' said Tom, looking at the barman.

Tom repeatedly punched his choices into the box until no

further free songs were available. He turned, both brothers on either side of him, and surveyed the room in front.

'Where's your lass?' asked Rich.

'She's still with the photographer, I think.'

'Oh, I'm sick o' that. Never endin'.'

Davy turned and whispered to his brother. Tom smiled as did Richie.

Jerry sat in the alcove in the cellar. Here in this space he had spent much of the last five decades thinking about his business and had watched his children come and go repeatedly until he was comfortably able to look on with pride at everything he had managed. Here, under the bar, and away from the limelight, he was able to reflect on the day, think of and look forward to the events later that evening. Nowhere in the building was he safer, or less accessible to the outside, and he relished, as he always had, the power and control he felt in his office, as he called it.

The burgundy leather covered desk behind which Jerry sat was piled at both ends with papers. Invoices and bills on the left were neatly filed into a blue leatherette ring-binder. These, which were next in line to be attended to, were a little too old for comfort, and on top of that was an envelope. He knew the contents of this envelope and hadn't opened it, despite the envelope dropping onto the porch floor three days earlier. At least it had been moved into its current position, he thought. It could wait until after the wedding.

A knock on the side of the alcove's side cladding – there was no need for a door to this little enclave, its being accessed only by those having already descended the ladder into the cellar.

'Dad. He's here.'

Davy surveyed his father. The old man sat squarely behind his desk in front of the green baize covered notice board next to three cardboard panels, the top of which revealed the left breast of a model beneath the pile of peanuts surrounding it. Her face, framed by a blonde bob and lit by the pictured sunshine, showed her wide smile. Blue pen gave the illusion that she was toothless top and bottom. The clock above Jerry's head, an old Budweiser sign, now without the neon light, showed 17:36 in red digits. New when it had arrived, the novelty of digital had soon worn off and this had been cast off into the inner sanctum. The filing cabinets, grey and austere, completed the cocoon into which his father could be found daily.

Jerry looked up. 'Show him doon, will you Davy? And where's Tommy? Bring him an' all.'

Davy retreated around the corner to the cooler door, back to the ladder and ascended slowly.

'Ye can gan doon noo.' Davy, addressing the man in the corridor, held open the hatch to allow him to descend and began to lower the hatch as he descended.

'Thanks.'

The gentleman, suited in black, red carnation in his left lapel, was mixing business with pleasure. Although he still had a little nervousness as he entered the cellar below, stepping from the bottom rung, he looked around, saw the cooler door and was reassured as he heard Jerry call him warmly from around the corner. Approaching, he noticed Jerry sat behind the desk – Regency Reproduction, a make of furniture popular throughout the North East. Jerry motioned to the chair in front of the desk, like a Captain inviting his lieutenant into his stateroom. The man grabbed the back of the chair, inserting his open hand upwards into the hand-hold making up the captain's chair. He pulled it back, straddled and settled comfortably into the chair. 'Canny,' he said.

'Well Mr Carlson, what can I do for you? Hope its worth my time on my niece's wedding day.'

Chapter 6

Davy pushed the pool-room door but it was unusually fastened from the inside, a table or something pushed in front to barricade it. He knocked loudly.

'Tom. Tom. Are you in there Son?'

He could hear the guests in the room opposite, and peering through the open doorway, Linda and Ian could be seen gazing into one another's eyes. The young woman, black shoulder length hair and olive skinned, was recognised as a local beauty set apart from the other girls and young women in the area by her Mediterranean looks – Sophia Loren her uncle called her. And she really looked great today. Then again, a bad lookout if she didn't wow today of all days.

He banged on the door again. The door opened slightly and Tom peered out. 'What do ye want? I'm busy.'

Tom looked over his shoulder and smiled, as did his brother.

'The Old Man is looking for you. He said he wants us both downstairs in the cellar.'

'Well, tell him I'll be down in a minute. Just a minute.'

'He's there noo. He's got Carlson there an' all.'

'Look, I'll be there in a minute.'

Davy looked past Tom's right shoulder and stared into the room. Their cousin Celia was bent over the pool table, naked from the waist down as her skirt was hitched up around her waist.

'Come on Tommy! Howay Baby.'

'Hiya Ce.' Davy turned and walked back down the corridor. Avoiding the cracks in the black and white chequered lino tiled floor, he paced slowly to the hatch before lifting it and climbing downwards.

'I've not seen you in here for well over a year, and you come in here noo askin' me to dig deep. Why? What's in it for us? For me?'

Carlson looked behind him as Davy moved in and seated himself to his left on an upturned red plastic Brown Ale crate placed there for the purpose of creating extra seating. He was keenly aware of the other and hoped his brother would soon take his place there. Ignoring the young man, Carlson addressed Jerry, informing the old man that today was a great day to begin a new venture. With the coming of age, so to speak, of his niece, and her new independence, now was a good time to put his first foot forward again. Everyone knew that business could be better for Jerry and he really should be thinking of branching out. Money's tight for everyone, but with Carlson's plan.

'Dad, sorry I'm late. Didn't know you were down here. Mr Carlson.' Tommy, breathless, bounded over to the desk and shook Carlson's hand before seating himself on the crate. Jerry smiled and motioned Carlson to carry on.

'Well, Jerry. A few blokes have been workin' down in Brough Park lately, and they've been offering me some pretty good tips. I've tried out a few of them and I can confirm that they have all, every one of them, been good. So far I have won over seventy quid with them. Just testing out, mind.'

'The dogs? Oh Aye?' Tommy's eyes lit as he thought of the last time he visited the dog track in Newcastle.

Jerry looked at his grandson nervously. If he could only

approach his gambling as he did the pool table maybe he'd fare better in the bookies. But this hot headed young buck couldn't contain his enthusiasm, preferring always to play to the gallery.

Carlson continued. He knew of a gang of lads in Newcastle who regularly slipped back handers to the handlers before they paraded the dogs out onto their places on the track. Before the dogs came out, the handlers would work some advantage. All Carlson was asking for was some money to get his venture properly underway, now that he knew the scheme was worthwhile. Perhaps twenty grand.

'What do you mean? Work some advantage? How?'

Carlson looked at the young man and smiled. 'Without going into too much detail Son, the dogs come out into the traps very happy.'

'What? You mean...?'

'Never mind what I mean, Son. Let's just leave it at that. But I can tell you that some of those dogs aren't going to want to do too much running after the handlers are finished with them.'

Davy looked at Tom and laughed.

'What, you mean they're hurtin' them, those poor dogs? What injectin' them?'

'Well, I'm sure that's sometimes how they do it. But this is a lot more humane. Givin' them extra food. Extra water. Failing that there are a couple o' lasses in Byker who, I'm told, are making race night much more enjoyable for them. And everyone's a winner. Leave it at that. There is also a lad in Gateshead.'

Tom looked at Davy before realisation registered on his face. The pair laughed. Jerry silenced them and asked Carlson to continue again.

'These 'handlers,' should we call them. They are paid off by the lads, no questions asked. Paid a bung and the dogs seem to lose interest in the rabbit. I have seen it myself. Mind they only do this a couple of times a month, and we can find out when.'

'What?' said Tom. 'You've seen these lasses...'

'Hoo Son, shut it will ye?' said Jerry. 'Don't be stupid. That's disgusting. He's not talkin' about that. He's talking about watching the races. Aren't you?'

'Yes,' answered Carlson with a snort of laughter. Everyone laughed before resuming.

'Listen Mr Carlson. This seems like it is a good plan and will probably make you some extra money. But for me, its a 'No.''

'What? You're joking aren't you Dad? I mean....'

Jerry looked at his eldest son. 'Shut up Son. What have I said?'

Tom's protestations slowly died out and Jerry went on:

'I'm sorry. He seems to think he can say whatever. Gets carried away with himself. His enthusiasm. And I've spoiled him.'

Davy turned away stifling a chuckle into the side of his clenched fist.

'No, Mr Carlson. I wish you all the best with all this. It should be good for you, but I can't afford to get mixed up in any nobbling, not like this. Gambling really isn't my bag, and I wouldn't like it to get out that I am involved in this. There are few enough customers coming in here as it is. If they thought I condoned that. Well.'

Jerry stood up and leaned over the desk. Right hand stretched out, Jerry warmly shook Mr Carlson's hand. His thumb pressed firmly into his host's knuckle, and Jerry reddened. Clearly distressed for some reason, Davy held out his hand to steady the old man. A moment later Jerry rejoined:

'I hope you will stay for a bite and celebrate the marriage of my niece Linda. Its a great day and we hope you'll enjoy yourself.'

Chapter 7

'Get away from here. Go on. Fuck off! Who the Hell do you think you are?'

'Look, my name's Davy Compton. I'm here on behalf of me dad. He's a reasonable man. Here's me number. Just give 'us a call. Anytime.'

Jones eyed the card in his hand and watched as Davy ambled away. A gang of youths mocked and laughed as Dave walked towards them, and the lamplight beamed over the drama set to unfold before him. Dave sauntered on, and eventually passed the small group congregating around the lamp-post. He paused and eyed the largest and laughed. Jones watched as the group began giggling. The big youth, isolated, looked around. Pondering, he decided to spit at Davy's feet before hurrying away. The group, his friends, whistled and jeered as Davy again sauntered on. A further fifty yards and he turned the key before he stooped and opened the car door. As the headlights came on the windscreen exploded with liquid, a well aimed egg hit the windscreen. The wipers angled over sweeping the mess amid thick jets of water. The engine coughed into gear and the car edged forward towards the group. Accelerating, the jeering and laughter rose to a crescendo as the Skoda swept past. Two hands slapped the side windows, one on each side. The aerial snapped and the car sped on. The big youth hurled a clod of earth in the car's wake. It fell short as the car turned and sped round the corner.

'Well done lads!' Jones waved in the group's direction and was greeted by further cheers. The bulb went out as one of the group aimed perfectly at the lamp.

'You know those kids, stupid kids, really. They need a good telling. I'm always out to them. Balls in the garden. Noise. The place is like a circus.'
'Look, I'm sorry I was a bit off with you the other night Davy. I just didn't realise you were speaking about the landlord. If I had known.'
'No worries Mr Jones. Not a problem'
'Ken. Call me Ken, Davy. Davy's alright, is it?'
Assenting, Dave entered the passageway of the home Ken Jones occupied. His dad's house by rights. He stepped over the threshold into the front room and walked through the small square space, fifteen feet by twelve, and into the back kitchen.
'Aye Davy, go on through, that's it. This is Imogen, me grand-daughter. Say "Hello" to Mr Compton, Imogen.'
Davy smiled politely as the young woman glanced up at him from her paper, 'The Sun.' Hair bundled into a knot at the back, dressed in a turquoise vest and white miniskirt she stretched her legs into her trainers below.
'I'd best be away Granddad. Gotta see Anna later. The bus is due.'
Dave nodded as the girl sidled past him and twisted round between him and the upright fridge freezer and out the door.
'Bye,' she said, as she met his gaze on the way out.
'Beautiful girl. I love that girl as if she was me own. Always wanted a daughter but ended up with a son. He's in the army and I hardly see him. But Imogen's down here plenty. Couldn't manage without her.'

'Yeah. She seems very nice.' Davy thought what it would be like meeting her in different circumstances. Would she maintain the innocence he had just seen, or would she put up a more spirited performance. He thought of Carlson, and how he would treat the young woman.

Jones opened a cupboard above the table as Davy sat down. Two glasses were placed on the tablecloth and they were half-filled with whisky. Davy liked White Horse, and he held up his glass. 'Imogen,' he toasted. Glasses chinked and the older man sat across from the younger. Davy shed his coat and put it around his chair back. He laid back politely and looked calmly at his host as he rose the glass to his lips.

'How is Jerry? I haven't seen him in years. Must be four, maybe five years. Great lad Jerry. I always liked him.'

Davy assured Jones that all was well with Jerry, and everyone connected with him and the Queen's Head. He also answered that the old man still fished regularly. And yes, he still had his portfolio of Northumbrian properties.

'Just like Jerry, that. All the houses were being vacated all over here after the strike ended. I mean, no one could afford to pay the rents. Jerry though. He knew a bargain. Snapped up a load of empty houses. This village and the next. He saved them really. Great bloke.'

Davy chatted, seemingly idly. He relaxed and drank another two shots from the now half empty bottle of White Horse. The pair, sussing one another, patiently enjoyed each other's company and the evening slowly transformed into night.

'Look Davy, I always liked Jerry, and we always had a mutual respect. But no, I'm afraid I really am not interested in leaving. Sorry, like.'

Davy shifted in his seat now that things were turning in a

more business like manner. He looked at Jones and tried to read him further. But nothing was hidden.

'Look Davy. I'm sure Jerry'll understand. I've lived here since I was a bairn. Not actually in this house, mind, but in this street. I've only ever lived in Widdrington, and the only way I'll be leaving here is in a box.' He winked at the younger man and laughed.

Davy swiftly joined in the polite laughter before rejoining that Jerry would see to it that Jones was very well looked after. 'With the money you'll get you could buy your own house, even twice the size, over in the next road. I mean, Jerry's a good friend to anyone whose willing to help him, you know that.'

Suddenly, Jones stood up, swigged the last of his whisky and stooped so his face was close to the seated younger man.

'Listen Son. I know all about this, and I am not for movin' I'm a sitting' tenant, and I kna me rights. I know Jerry is wanting all the hooses in this street, but he isn't getting this one. This is mine. Too many memories, and I 'm too old for the upheaval My mother died in the room upstairs, and I can't move. Sorry.'

About to try a different tack, Davy was shocked when the old man shouted for him to get out. The belligerence of their first meeting had returned and he felt embarrassed as well as uncomfortable.

'Dye mind if I call a taxi? I came by bus, and God knows when the next one'll be around here.'

'I couldn't give a monkey's Son. Just get your coat and sod off out of here. You can tell Jerry I said "Hello." And he can stick he's money. I'm not being pushed out like the rest of them round here. Just get out. Now!'

Davy picked up his coat and hurried out through the front

room, the corridor and out into the street. Sleet blew around in the freezing air, lamppost beams highlighting the blustering flakes. He hurried away, avoiding the group standing by the light.

'Hold on. Hold on a minute!'
Jones ran down the stairs fastening the tasselled rope around his dressing gown as he reached the foot of the stairs.
'Hang on Jack. I'll be there in a minute.'
The door opened and Jack, the postman, stood with a package below his delivery clipboard.
'Here Ken. Sign here, will you?'
'What's this?' Jones' rhetorical question directed not at the postman but a thought out loud. He signed alongside the bottom sticker – a barcode on a thin orange strip.
'There you go Son.'
Inside Ken opened the package and found a boxed video. Resembling a classic book, the case was opened and he surveyed the blank tape. No clues as to what was on it, or from whom it came.
'Bloody rubbish!' he tossed it to one side and entered the kitchen. He switched on the kettle before pondering further on the video and its mysterious contents.

Returning with a mug of tea and a bacon stottie, Ken opened the video case and pulled out the tape before bending down and peering at the video controls. Picking up the remote control, he slid the tape into the slot, heaved himself up and fell back onto the settee behind him. His belly-fat rolling out of his dressing gown, which had loosened itself, rippled as he bounced onto the seat.
'Let's see now.'

He peered closely at the remote before pressing play.

'Where's me glasses?' he asked himself aloud as the video hummed and the TV screen went blue. 'SP' followed by the date and time of the video. Two weeks ago.

Imogen sat on a ruffled bed in a darkened room, spotlight shining on her as a syringe was pulled from inside her elbow by an unknown hand. A man's hand held up a newspaper; a three week old copy of the *Hull Daily Mail*. Bright red lipstick smeared across her left cheek. She smiled. Dried black mascara streamed down her cheeks. She looked into the camera, waved, blew a kiss and said 'Hello Granddad. Love you.'

The camera zoomed out and two men, naked but for their masks, a clown and The Incredible Hulk, approached her from either side as she stretched out and reached for both their erections and kissed them, one at a time. She winked into the camera before laying back on the crumpled sheets.

Chapter 8

The hotel lounge bar, as always, was empty when Siobhan entered. She had been permitted by the receptionist out front to take a look at the hotel's piece de resistance.

The sinking of the Titanic, possibly the most famous ocean liner in history, had spurred on countless books and stories about the world's most luxurious ship. It was amazing to imagine that in a town in rural Northumberland it was possible to get a taste of the opulence once enjoyed by those on that fateful journey halfway to America.

Alnwick's White Swan had managed to procure lounge fittings of the Titanic's sister ship. The similarly ill fated Olympic, like the titanic, was built in Northern Ireland. However, its end came not in the romantic story in the Atlantic, but ignominiously decades later in the dry docks of the Tyne. With its close proximity to the ship yards and dry docks of Newcastle and Wallsend the RMS Olympic was broken up, scrapped and parts sold off to those interested.

Holding the leaflet, Siobhan stood by the dimly lit empty bar and read the printed paper in front of her. Looking at the bubble jet printed sheet of A4, she questioned why more was not made of this gem.

> The Olympic Suite's panelling, mirrors, ceiling and stained glass windows were removed from the RMS Olympic when she

was being dismantled in Jarrow in 1936. The hotel's then-owner, Allenton Smart, had been a frequent traveller on Olympic and took part in the auction of the ship's fittings in November 1935. At the auction, which was run by the London firm Knight Frank & Rutley, he had the winning bids for elements of the First Class Lounge, the Aft First Class Staircase, and the revolving door from the liner's restaurant.

Like so much in the North East, history seemed taken for granted. She knew, if this was anywhere else, this would be a visitor attraction teeming with American tourists. Was it modesty or just stupidity that stunted the locals' enterprising nature? Once the greatest ship building area in the world, why had so much changed for the worst. Indeed, the phrase taking coals to Newcastle. That was almost a mockery now. No one wanted coal now, and this area, and Tyneside thirty miles to the south, was a sorry casualty to the movement of globalisation and international trade. It had all moved on now. But why didn't the people here make more of this, and attractions like it?

Her husband, with so much in his favour, could never see himself as she always did. 'Confidence was key,' he told his students at every opportunity in inspiring their efforts. If only he heeded his own advice. If he took a good look at his own reflection and applied himself in kind. What they could achieve!

The First Class Lounge on Olympic was identical to that of her sister ship Titanic; both were designed and fitted by the same teams of craftsmen and artisans, as the two ships were constructed at the same time only yards apart. The interiors of the ships were designed by Adam, Heaton & Co, who had previously worked on other White Star Line vessels and had also carried out interior design on the homes of White Star Line chairman J. Bruce Ismay and his family.

Was it just bad luck? Had these people, her husband's people, just been unlucky? Had they been superseded by other people in other countries? Their local knowledge and evident skills forsaken by a setting sun moving to the new multi-million dollar industries further afield. The war, surely it had taken its toll, but there had been life in the area even afterwards.

Before? No. She knew, just as in Ulster, there had been hardships then. The Depression. Did that mean the war, with its booming economy, a saviour of the shipyards and industry everywhere, had been good for the area? Inevitably though, the decline had come and life, strangulated by poverty and neglect, ground....

Siobhan flipped open the phone and answered:

'Hi. I'm in the White Swan. Interesting. The Olympic Lounge. Nobody here but me. How's Aidan? Where are you? Lovely town this.'

'OK. Yeah, he's fine. We're coming back in a bit. Just getting some shopping and exploring a bit.

'OK. Yeah. See you in an hour.'

The equivalent lounge on Titanic was described by The Shipbuilder magazine as a

> place where, during voyages, "passengers will indulge in reading, conversation, cards, tea-drinking and other social intercourse." It disintegrated during Titanic's sinking, releasing many wooden fragments to float to the surface while strewing metal fittings across the sea bed.

I hope he's alright, she thought.

> An archway from the lounge preserved at the hotel is identical to the same archway from Titanic which was recovered by ships from Halifax, Nova Scotia searching for bodies and is now displayed at the Maritime Museum of the Atlantic in Halifax.

Black as always.

Rippling coffee surface, the short mug, lifted from the saucer, glided to Siobhan's lips.

Slurp.

'This is how we test the flavour and texture.'

Big soup spoon, dipped again. Different pot. Slurp.

Couldn't go that far. Cold coffee. Liked it like this though. Espresso.

The mug returned to the saucer. Siobhan lifted the little pot, dropped steaming inky liquid back into the little mug. Relax.

Siobhan lifted the paper towards her and read.

> Police are investigating an incident at a Tynedale farm after 20 lambs were killed.
>
> A spokeswoman for Northumbria Police

said the force received a report of sheep worrying at Gill Farm, Haltwhistle, between Wednesday night and Thursday morning.

Six lambs and three ewes were also injured.

Anyone with any information is asked to Northumbria Police on 0191 8645093, quoting log 35664473.

Hexham Courant. Courant? A bird. Like a shag? Weird name for a paper.
Northumberland Gazette. Better name.

Suspected fuel thieves arrested in Northumberland.

Four suspected fuel thieves were arrested after a suspicious vehicle was spotted in Northumberland.

Wednesday

Northumbria Police received a report of a suspicious vehicle parked near Alnwick just after 11.50pm on Tuesday.
Upon closer inspection, officers found a teenager sleeping and several large fuel containers in the back of the burgundy Land Rover. Officers conducted a search of the area an soon located three men, 35, 27 and 21, all smelling strongly of fuel.

Following further inquiries the three men and the sleeping female teen, 18, were arrested on suspicious of theft.

Chief Inspector Ted Marving, said: 'This is great work by local rural officers who acted on their instincts and as a result we now have four people in our cells.'

'Their quick actions ensured a timely and effective response which has reassured the community that thefts of any kind will be swiftly.....'

She folded the paper and carefully placed it into her bag, pulled out her purse and laid a fiver down in the ashtray by the empty unused ice bucket. A small donation, miniscule in comparison to the value this room, its atmosphere ghostly and macabre, provided during this drizzly Wednesday afternoon.

Turning, she took a final look at the panelled walls and fluted pillars, oddly stark and surely a disappointment to anyone travelling the White Star Line in 1912. She pushed the revolving door and walked through the carousel.

'Thanks again.'

The receptionist smiled before returning to her monitor.

Siobhan picked up the phone and looked at her messages. Two new:

Accident compensation
You have still not claimed the compensation you are due for the accident you had. To start the process please reply YES. To opt out text STOP.

'Where do they get the numbers for these texts? Junk

everywhere.'

'Siobhan, Dads in hospital. They've taken him to the RVI. I need to get there but where are you?

She dialled, waited and no answer.
Again; no answer.
Contacts – Queen's Head. She dialled the pub.
'Hello, Queen's Head, Amble.'
'Hello, Gillian.'
'Oh, Siobhan, is that you? Look Jerry's been rushed into hospital. He's in Newcastle – the RVI. Are you anywhere near?'
'I'm in Alnwick. Where's Colin? Is he with you? Has he gone to Newcastle. Has he got Aidan?'
'He's on his way, but he only just left. The bairn's here with us. He's fine. No-one went with Jerry. They had to call an ambulance from Morpeth. He was out shopping. I think Richie may have been with him, but we're not sure. Can't get hold of him.'
'Well I'll head straight there. I have the car. I should make it in about an hour. OK, Bye.'
Siobhan flipped the faux leather case on her mobile, like a wallet after an important purchase.

Chapter 9

'Prodigy!'

Col pulled out the bend, changed up and accelerated towards the corner ahead. Third? The left moved to shift back down. Braking at the last second, the car slowed then turned the L-bend and onward. The left again changed up - direct into fourth.

The road stretched ahead as the Carlton accelerated down the hill. Sea below, blue horizon below a blue sky. The grey line ahead, bordered by hedgerow, bordered green fields to the right, deciduous forest left.

Tape blared. Surround sound. Sony all round.

Bass banged. Car sped. Down hill. Up the clock in front. Faster. Faster. The road began to even out and the sea, blue wedge, more and more acute, began to retreat beneath the hedge right.

Red sports car in front – hurtling toward him. Blonde! Knew it.

Around the long undulated bend, behind two more, saloon, white, estate – old bloke – red. Into third, as the road stretched straight. He accelerated. Forty, forty-five, fifty, sixty, seventy eighty-four. He moved back into the left, in front a lorry, HGV, Confederacy, British Hill-Billy type, Scots flag on the reg. Idiot! Sunglasses stared ahead at him.

What is the point of slow driving? Exhilarating, fast driving raised the pulse, it excited and was a means of getting about quickly.

Not so long ago, travel was nowhere. A day from Newcastle to Alnwick.

Granddad lost his lass on the way home. Nineteen, on a date to Rothbury and back. Side car – all the rage – it detached near Morpeth. She went home on a different bike. Different bloke. Oil and two bolts found in the yard back home. Some engineer. Long before he'd served his time. Who'd a thought it? Best engineer o the Tyne. Was he Parson?

Dad had said a bloke who worked with his dad once said 'Jack. You know him do you? 'Aye, I know him' said Dad. 'Jack's the best engineer on the Tyne.'

Not that good on the way to Rothbury though. Eh?

He could always tell the tale, mind. Aye, plenty of tales. Porkies, more like.

'Look up the mountains and wait 'til you see the whites of their eyes.'

I used to look at that picture for hours. Granddad glued to Grandstand, or ITV Sport – racing, Rugby. Whatever. I use to stare – 'There Granddad. There's one.'

The septuagenarian, just turned, would glance from the black and white screen, 'No, keep looking.' Tiresome, must have been, but it never showed.

Strange how different Granddad Wilson was from Jerry's side o' the family. Different people. Worlds apart.

Down to second, brake. The bend hurtled forwards Colin, almost to a stop. Third, thirty, forty, fifty, sixty and then seventy. At last! Back into fifth. Great!

Road twisted ahead. Hedgerow either side, the two lanes, white lines, long, short breaks, narrowed as the road snaked away from the windscreen.

Colin lifted his hand from the wheel. Dropped it to the button, silver triangle (forward). He slowly counted as the fast forward whirred. One, two, three, four.

'Brilliant!'

The tape settled into the last of the 3 tracks. Colin's favourite driving style. The best tracks, continuous, for the last of the journey ahead.

Back on the road, only a glance away, but the bend loomed. Brake!!!!

The car halted. Emergency stop. No damage. Near miss.

Neutral. Clutch, first, second, third, clutch, second, corner, third, fourth, forty, fifty, sixty. Fifth.

Pumping, the beats blared and Colin's pulse raced. Adrenaline.

So lucky. Never had this in those days. What would Granddad have thought of this?

Chapter 10

'I'm here to inquire about Jerry Compton. Is he alright?'
Siobhan stared at the book splayed in front of the woman behind the desk, cocooned in the office behind the glass screen. At anytime she could just slide that glass and no one would be able to bother her. No, she looked like she cared.

'Let me see. You are? Yes, his daughter-in-law. Yes. We had him come in earlier. Ambulance from Morpeth. Yes, he is in intensive care. I'm afraid you can't see him now. You'll have to wait. Its immediate family only. And anyway, visiting doesn't start until seven.'

'But he's my father-in-law. Can't I see him for just a minute. What about his family? Is anyone with him now?'

'Look, I don't know. I am sorry. Perhaps make enquiries on the ward. Yeah. Up on the fifth floor. You can't go in though.'

Siobhan turned and wafted through the corridor and the smokers. Zombies in nighties and dressing gowns. Some of the girls looked like that anyway – oh, that's not fair.

The corridor, fluorescent lit, strip lit, following the blue guide duct, supposedly to buffer and guide the beds, but now a kind of yellow-brick road to the lift. Despite this people in civvies lost and confused, clustering round signs.

Toilets – man and woman, disabled pictures.

Triage -X-ray – Maternity – Exit

Each junction with its hub of signage, instead of pointing directions seemed to further the confusion all were feeling. Until the staff, in white coats or nurses' uniforms could point the way and lead to enlightenment. But only if asked. Generally, open coated, tweed or suede jacketed men, fashionably clad women, white coats open like capes glided past, spectacled, stethoscoped, moving in the right direction. Always in the opposite direction. Dinner, lunch. Tired out. Busy and focused.
'Do you know where ICU is?'
'What Luv? What?'
'Intensive care. My father-in-law is in intensive care. Heart attack, I think.'
'Oh. I don't know Pet. Me Mam's only an outpatient.'
'Thanks.'
Better not to ask around. No one seems to have a clue.
Siobhan joined the gathering awaiting the lift. Three huge double-doors in a wide atrium; well lit silence. She looked around. Blonde whispering to her sister, mother in a wheelchair, cigarette stink and brown nicotine stained fingers. Smiling, a man caught her eye momentarily, then looked down staring at the blue screed floor. Ding. Arrived.
The queue, as it would be known anywhere else, shuffled into the cavernous room. The man, looking round politely, pressed the square indicating level three.
'Two,' the woman in the wheelchair coughed, rasping into her handkerchief. 'Five.' Siobhan reached over obsequiously and without offence pushed the button corresponding to her choice – guess.
The man, looked down at the grey linoleum tiles covering

the floor.

'Mam, what are they givin' you for dinner?'

'Lamb dinner. Horrible. Wouldn't give it to King. Gravy.'

'What not nice, is it?'

'The puddin's a'reet, but you can't have pop.' I need me Coke. Costs a fortune here. Kelly, run oot and get me some, will ye? Not Pepsi. Unless there's nowt else. And not Diet either.'

'Mam. You're in hospital. You should take it easy.'

'Kelly, I need me Coke. Naebody knows what's good for me like me, that's what I say. I'll be glad to get back hyem. Sooner the better!'

The silence returned before the doors parted. The ladies alighted and the doors, opened momentarily, closed and the floor moved upward. The lift shook slightly as it ascended. The man looked and smiled shyly. Siobhan smiled back. The door opened again. She was alone.

Exiting, Siobhan looked around at the gathering people, 'Is this ICU?'

'No, you need the fifth floor. You're on the fourth. Should have got off on the next.'

Embarrassed, Siobhan smiled at the waiting doctor. Dark skinned Whitney, hair flowing -

> ... Oh! I wanna dance with somebody
> I wanna feel the heat with somebody
> Yeah! I wanna dance with somebody
>   With somebody who loves me ...

'Oh, I pressed..'

'Aye, I kna. That happens a lot.' Whitney smiled and entered the lift. Geordie Whitney. Broad Geordie. Amazing the accents that keep coming out of people's mouths here. Just like Albert.

Hard man. Or so she thought. Typical Belfast hard man. Grizzled and unshaven, except his short crew cut hair. Hooped Celtic shirt, replica, and black 501s. Maybe not Celtic. Brogues, brown. Broad Belfast. Unintelligible. Ian had introduced her to this hard man, and said he was one of the most promising artists to come out of Barcelona in the last ten years. Studying at Ulster University Fine Arts department. Catalan. Or is it Catala. Occitane. Unintelligible!

'Here we are. If you turn left and go straight to the end of the corridor you'll see it. You'll have to buzz. Someone'll let you in. The lift closed. Whitney left. Meeting Geordie Bobby Brown.

'Afraid its family only. '

'But I am family. I'm Mr Compton's daughter-in-law.'

'Sorry. Direct family only.'

'But please. I have just driven from Alnwick. I got here as quickly as possible. Has he got anyone else with him?'

'Sorry. This is intensive care. We haven't got room. You'll have to wait outside.'

The nurse smiled and brushed her shoulder sympathetically, turned and exited the area into a small office. Alone, heart racing, Siobhan proceeded through the open door and looked around the ward. Beeping and the sound of ventilators. Breathe!!

Splayed and drooling, eyes unseeing, a man seemed to be staring into the corner, framed by the olive and white striped curtain pulled around and hiding his neighbour and room-mate. A window, picturing the grey monotony of windows and black wall outside, illuminated the bed next to it, to which Siobhan darted in silent guilty approach. Terrified of discovery, yet determined to uncover Jerry, she peered down. A man, also in his later years, tried to raise a cannula pierced hand. Siobhan retreated and opened the curtains. Jerry Compton lay, open mouthed and silent. Asleep. One arm pinned to the bed by swirling wires and another trailing, his left hand palm down pointing at the floor – more screed.

Siobhan looked at the frail figure. Aged a generation, this was no longer the man who'd haul fishing nets and heavy kegs with ease. Ashen, grey and wrinkled, hair matted above the washed out striped jacket of his pyjamas, Siobhan knew this was the same man, her husband's dad, nevertheless, he was altered. Different and a shell of his former self. In 24 hours, since she had last seen him, he had gained a score of years. How was Colin going to take this change? How were his brothers going to fare?

'Excuse me. I told you you could not come in here. You aren't allowed. I am going to have to ask you to leave.'

Siobhan jumped in fright. Arrested by fear and feeling the guilt of her intrusion, she tried to formulate a response, some kind of excuse. Nothing came forth, and she mumbled an apology. The nurse, sternly grabbed her arm, then smiled on exiting through into the corridor.

'I know it is hard Pet. I know that. But we can't cope with all the visitors in here. Its an ICU, but it'd be a football match if all the visitors came in whenever they felt like it. We have to be strict. Apart from the difficulty of managing everyone in here, and administering the meds, there is the dignity of patients. That's why we insist on immediate fam....'

'I know you are family Pet. But please. Can you please just wait outside? Better still go and get yourself a coffee, or a cup of tea. As you can see, your father-in-law is in a

bad way, but he'll probably feel better tomorrow, and he is in the right place here. Look, I'll add you to the list of family members authorised to visit. You can come in at seven. Not sure for how long yet, but we'll see.'
Siobhan smiled, tears welling – not for the tragedy of Jerry's situation – but of frustration and embarrassment at being caught. Thanks muttered, smiling, Siobhan exited the door – button, rounded and green, and out. Her embarrassment and fear ebbed as she progressed towards the lift and the real world outside.

Chapter 11

'Siobhan? Siobhan. It is you. Well what ye daein' here?'
Siobhan looked up from her crossword and noticed the blonde. Mohair sweater to her chin, platinum blonde atop, hooped leggings below and above red high heels.
'Celia. Hello. How are you?'
'Oh, OK.' Celia sat down and placed her drink on the table next to Siobhan's coffee, now cold.
'I'm waiting to go back into the hospital. Jerry's taken in this afternoon. No one is with him. He's in intensive care.'
'What. Oh God. Is he alright?'
'Well, I have seen him and he was asleep. I sneaked in and feel terrible about it.'
'Celia rose and walked over to the bar. Trend setting and hip, the menu board above the tiled back listed dozens of drinks and cocktails. Chalked in white or scrawled in marker pen, Pina Colada stood out – buy one get one free. The barman emptied the pre-mixed drinks into the cocktail glasses – fruit slaked and flooded by creamy white.
'What a shame. He's gonna be alright then, d'ye think?'
Celia took a long draught from the straight glass and picked out a pineapple chunk. Sucking and licking it as she listened.
The barman approached and placed another two straight half pint glasses on Brown Ale emblazoned table mats.
'Thanks Hun,' answered Celia. 'He's a bit of alright, eh?'

Beaming, chuckling, she pulled up her heels and tucked them under her hooped leggings.

'So, what d'ye think Siobhan? C'mon, drink up.'

Although Siobhan was puzzled as to the sincerity of the young woman's questions, and her seeming obliviousness as to Siobhan's predicament with regards driving her car back to Amble, it soon became clear that Celia, far from being uncaring, was all ears. But she punctuated every situation with lots of strong alcohol. In this case, such was the severity of the situation with her uncle, that she was even more liberal in her libations. The third round came before Siobhan fully understood how the young woman had always loved Jerry, the pub, and had spent many hours from the age of fourteen behind the bar when on holiday.

'Jerry, he's the bollocks.' Celia leaned in further, resting her head on the older woman's shoulder and stared at the barman.

'Rob, can we have another two please? This time, we'll have tequila sunrises.'

Siobhan had relaxed considerably and felt the Trent House enliven. Why a pub on Tyneside, in Newcastle city centre, should be called so, she had no idea. But she could see and feel its atmosphere, its ambiance. As the bar became less and less empty, as the music began to signify, all unknown tracks and tunes, but amplified and relevant no less, Siobhan felt that she was beginning to get to know Celia, her lifestyle and this city – the Toon. The two women, so obviously different in so many ways; one a bold young woman from Northumberland; the other, a soft spoken Irishwoman. Celia in her late teens, Siobhan almost thirty, the former without any responsibilities, Siobhan with her husband and child,

Aidan. Both were bonding and it seemed as if this bond was to be an unbreakable one. Siobhan poured the remains of the screwdriver into her mouth, crunched the ice loudly, drowning the music and conversation as she did so. Celia handed her the Zombie.

'Cheers!'

Their glasses clinked and both laughed, and hugged each other.

'Jerry, he's like everybody's fatha'. A lovely old uncle. My great uncle.' Again, 'Cheers.'

Siobhan's hand was pulled and she found herself lunging to the bar. She steadied herself and looked as Celia pulled her to the middle of the room. Pushed, Siobhan fell back before her wrists were once again wrenched back. She steadied herself. In front of her Celia twisted and twirled, jumping up and down, marching back and forth, in and out of the circle. She was running around the older woman. Responding, Siobhan steadied herself consciously before shuffling and jumping. Dancing. It had started now and Siobhan felt alive and knew the evening was about to begin for real. But she had to remember why she was waiting. Jerry, across in the hospital. After another round, the ladies drank up, said goodbye to the people around them, and headed outside. Arm in arm they walked and chatted their way to the hospital entrance.

'I think you're relaxin' noo Siobhan. Are you feelin' happier?'

'Yes – Aye.' They both laughed and stepped out into the road, stopping a car, lights making a mild impression on the dimming twilight pink lustre descending on the city. Parallel, alongside Leaze's Park, the women headed to the Leaze's entrance and to the bed of their relative, both heading towards the head of their family, and Siobhan felt a love for this man, a paternal love that she had never experienced with her own father. She knew that this old man, lonely and dishevelled, or seemingly so, was the centre of a world she was now coming to understand, one which she had been thrust into today. She knew that this sense of belonging, unfelt a few hours ago, had been spelled out for her by her new friend, and relative. She felt overwhelmed with gratitude and love.

At the entrance to the hospital, Siobhan and Celia stopped.

'I'll meet you in a bit. I hate hospitals. I'll be in the Strawberry. It's just ower there. See? St James's Park. There. Its just opposite. Great pub. Should be heaving noo. I'll see you there in a bit. Are you OK?'

'Yes Celia. But don't you want...'

Celia demurred, excused herself and added that she would be waiting for her when visiting was over.

'Tell Jerry I said "Hi." That I love him, and I'm gonna give him a big kiss next week.'

In the lift Siobhan thought that she may be a little early. Then again, if so, she could hang around for a few minutes. She thought of going back to the cafe but decided to proceed.

'I am afraid it is direct family only Mrs Compton. I am afraid you are going to have to wait until Mr Compton is transferred out of intensive care.'

'But I spoke with the nurse earlier. She said she would add me to the list of those authorised to visit my father-in-law. She said she would do that here about half-three.'

'I'm sorry, I know nothing of that. You'll have to come back when he's been transferred.'

'Siobhan, have you seen him yet?

Siobhan turned from the nurse to see her husband rushing down the corridor towards them. Usually embarrassed by his loud voice in social situations, and much preferring social decorum, she was happy that he was here to intervene on this occasion.

The nurse looked on as Colin approached.

'I'm here to visit my dad. Jerry Compton. Is this the ward he's on?'

The nurse turned to Colin and ignoring his wife, said that Jerry was indeed in the unit.

'Are you immediate family?' She went on to add that he would be admitted in five minutes. 'Visiting is from seven pm 'til eight. I was just explaining to your wife that it is immediate family only. I'm afraid she will have to wait outside.'

The nurse turned to Siobhan.

'I know he is your father-in-law but...'

Before Colin could argue Siobhan said:

'Don't worry Colin. She's not worth it. I'll meet you later. I am off to meet Celia in the pub. I met her earlier. I'll see you in The Strawberry afterwards. Its opposite the football ground.'

Chapter 12

CLACK – C-LACK!!!'
'Look at that – what a shot!'
Tom quickly looked up and over the green baize down the table towards the top pocket. Up and down, his head bobbed, winking, dodging and weaving. Anyone would be forgiven for thinking that he was in an elaborate shadow box, rather than in his regular workout at the pool table. He hit the cue hard, the orange five went straight into the top corner. He rose, chalked the cue, his beloved Riley, and he paced slowly round the table, backwards and forwards he rocked on his left foot, staring down and onward to the top right.
'Dad is stable. Just had Siobhan on the phone.'
'Great.'
Replying, Tom stopped looking at the table and turned in the door's direction and at Dave.
'Has she seen him? What about Colin?'
'Colin's in the hospital now. She said she sneaked in to see him earlier and got a glimpse of him earlier. She got thrown out. Direct family only.'
Tom looked across at the clock. Seven-twenty.
With Jerry ill in hospital everyone looked to Tom, his heir apparent, to take control of the ongoing situation. It was fortunate that Dave, his brother, was also on hand to reign in the young man and ensure an even handed approach to the needs of the pub, especially in the light of current financial constraints. That was how the Old Man

wanted things. Although there was massive mutual love and respect between these two young men, almost inseparable in many ways, age one of these key commonalities, there was also a key difference. While Tom was undoubtedly the charismatic one, it was Davy who embodied the judgement and prudence necessary to managing the pub.

'We need to get people to understand he's in trouble. We need to get people out and into the pub so we can let him know how missed he is,' said Tom. 'I think the best thing is to get the pool league involved. We should have a special tournament. Like a testimonial.'

Dave sat down at the table next to his brother and smiled.

'Do you think Dad wants everyone to know he is hurt. That's not his style Tom.'

'Well he's not here is he? Who knows what's gonna happen to him? All we can do is hope for the best. And this will show us who our friends are.'

Dave looked at Tom and, the smile never leaving his face, added that a pool tournament, which everyone would probably take part in, would not make things better. In fact, when their dad returned from hospital there was nothing to say it would not have made the situation worse.

'The Old Man really doesn't like people seeing he's in trouble. He has always been the one to give help to his friends. I think that's how we should carry on. Just play this cool. And anyway, we a'ready kna who he's friends are.'

'Cool?' Tom jumped up from the seat and stared down at Dave.

'That's the problem here. How can we play it cool? We need a proper manager now.'

Dave, piqued by the obvious reference to their different outlooks and temperaments, suddenly reddened. The smile no longer visible as tears welled.

'Look Dave. I'm sorry. I didn't mean that. Just ignore me. I divn't kna what I'm on about. I take it back.' Tom walked over and hugged his brother.

'We shouldn't be arguing. Not noo.'

Dave stood up and hugged in return.

'I'm off to see Gillian. She's in the kitchen. Martin's on the bar.'

'Aye. Martin. He's a good 'un.'

Tom remained in the pool room to continue his practice, but he couldn't concentrate as he would normally. He returned to the seat and sipped from his whisky and Coke.

'I'll get a double next,' he thought, pouring the rest of the Coke into the small glass.

'I wasn't allowed in. They said I had to be immediate family and, even though I told them he's my father-in-law, I had to wait outside. I actually went over to meet with Celia. Met by accident but met her later again in the pub. Colin went in by himself and met us later.'

Siobhan did not elaborate on the argument she and her husband had on the way home. He was not happy with her mixing with Celia, who he thought a bad influence.

Gillian cut the carrots into the pot, boiling and emitting steam throughout the galley kitchen. Onions, carrots and pieces of minced beef rising and falling within.

'We're having a tournament. Tryin' to get the locals to come in and spend some of their hard earned, as alwi's.'

'Do the locals know that Jerry's in hospital? That he's in intensive care.'

'Dave thought it best not to let everyone kna aboot it. So we just told them he was in for a routine operation. Nothing to do with he's heart.'

Siobhan sprinkled salt and pepper into the pot before walking over to the end of the room.

'What you doing now?'

Siobhan, looking at the bowl in Gill's hand, watched as she placed it below the wall unit and took two kilo bags of flour from inside.

'We are giving away mince and dumplin's. Everyone loves this, and it should help draw in the players. We always have this on tournament nights. Always make it the neet afore.'

Gillian sprinkled the suet and mixed, turning the large round wide rimmed basin as she kneaded. 'Never put too much water in at first.'

Gill poured in a half pint of water, mashed the dough with a wooden spoon and poured in another half pint. Mixing, the dough quickly congealed and Siobhan looked at the steaming pot.

'Oh, we'll put this in in a minute. Best to leave it stand. Dumplin's are lush. An' they'll thicken it up. Has to be self-raisin' though.'

Gill sprinkled the dough with more of the flour before lifting the basin and shaking it to form the dough into a ball.

'I'll cut that into smaller pieces afore I drop it into the mince. Pan Hagglety. Just like me Nana's. We'll also have pies and sausage rolls. We buy them in mind. Not worth makin' ourselves. Everybody'll lap it up.'

Chapter 13

The gloom was settling over the city. The Toon, as many called it. Davy walked down the bank and headed for the Haymarket. The terraced houses on either side had recently been cleaned and made up what was to become one of Newcastle's major regeneration projects. The roar from St James's Park pierced through the drizzle and Davy headed around the corner and along the railings toward the pelican crossing.

'Davy! Davy, Davy Compton!'

He looked over the road in the direction of the voice and saw Carlson standing there. He smiled and waved and joined the group heading over the road. The pelican beeped intermittently as they headed across. He was surrounded by umbrellas, black trad, blue fold-away and a hemispherical polythene dome through which a young woman peered above an upturned undulating wave of shiny fabric. Carlson awaited him on the other side. Davy held out his hand in greeting and they smiled at one another as the crowd's voice rose again, this time the roar lingered.

'Looks like one nil then.'

Davy nodded in smiled agreement.

'What you up to Davy? Hear your dad's in hospital.'

Davy wondered at Carlson's knowledge. Only a few family members knew the true nature of Jerry's hospitalisation. Although it was common knowledge in and around the pubs and clubs of Amble that Jerry had been taken into hoapital, Davy was surprised that news had reached Carlson.

'Fancy a quick pint Davy?'

'Oh, I can't Ronnie. I was just visiting me dad. Gotta get back and don't want to miss the bus.'

'What? There'll be another bus along in an hour. Plenty of time for a pint. I'll get them in Man.'

Davy knew this was a demand rather than a request, although he would be sure to get his turn in. 'Alright.'

He indicated The Percy, back over the crossing from whence he'd just come. He leant around the post and pressed the button on the console. 'WAIT' illuminated the gloom as water droplets bounced off its top and rain splashed on the ground. Carlson took the young man's arm and the two men hesitated until the beeping resumed and they, with another flat-capped man, walked in the direction of the group headed towards them. Meeting in the road, Davy avoided a young woman with a buggy, headlights emphasising the rainfall as droplets splashed off the polythene covering the child beneath.

'He looks alright, eh?'

Carlson smiled at the push chair. The woman beamed back as they passed each other.

'Wouldn't get many o' them in a pound Davy.'

Despite the advancing years of his companion, it was clear that Carlson still maintained his sexual appetite, one which Davy had heard knew no boundaries where age was concerned.

The bar was busy but it would be another quarter of an hour before the crowd from St James's swelled its number.

'Just in time to get a seat,' said Carlson. 'What you having?'

'I'll have Exhibition, Ronnie.'

Davy pulled up a stool and sat down at the table. He settled into the atmosphere, the mahogany fixtures of the bar, above and below, sheening amidst the brass and cut frosted glass panels The carpet, newly laid, still smelled new. The commentary on the radio was barely audible amidst the raised voices of two companions at the side of the bar furthest from the door.

'Shut up, Man, will ye?'

Davy looked down and reached over to the stool at the next table.

'D'ye mind if I have a look at yer *Chronicle* please?'

As agreed, Davy scanned the front page quickly and then opened the broadsheet further and looked inside.

Innocent dogs being drugged in rigged races, Trainers quizzed.

In a two-month undercover investigation, *The Evening Chronicle* has discovered that greyhounds are given dangerous drugs to make them run either faster or slower. The illegal practice means races can then be fixed – with huge profits coming from betting on the rigged outcomes.

This drugging of defenceless animals is openly talked about on the greyhound circuit.

We caught one greyhound trainer on video boasting how he deliberately slowed down his dogs in order to rig races to get better odds.

Richard Benny, 50, said he used

> prescription-only valoids to slow down his racing animals. Keen to cash in, he then made arrangements to get one for our reporter, who was posing as someone looking to get involved in the sport.
>
> Valoids are a human drug used to treat vertigo and should only be given out by a doctor. Never to animals.
>
> Benny said: "Give me a list. If I can't get it here, I'll get it in Ireland. I go over to Ireland every couple of weeks. Anything you need – injections or anything – I'll get it."

Davy turned the broadsheet over.

> Greyhound racing – The tactics that can win races but kill dogs
>
> Valoids have the chemical name of Cyclizine and are an anti-histamine drug given to treat humans for vomiting, nausea and dizziness. But in racing dogs they are used to sabotage performance – with reckless disregard for the dog's welfare.

'Interesting story, eh Davy?'

The younger man looked up as Carlson placed their two drinks before them on the rectangular table. Davy respected Carlson, and the fact he was also an Exhibition drinker further endeared him.

'Good pint?' he asked.

'No. Not really. But its a coincidence that you're here when I'm reading this article, mind. Its about the dogs.

The corruption and cruelty involved. To think, we were just on about that last time we met up.'

Carlson took a long draw from his large glass and looked straight at Davy's eyes from above the brim.

'There's two sides to everything. You just get one slant with that. I know there are plenty people involved in dog racing who are neither corrupt nor cruel. There's a lot more like that than the bent ones anyway.'

'Ye know that Greyhound racing goes back to Ancient Egypt. They used t' meet and race the dogs in much the same way as we do. There 's a lot we could learn from Ancient Egypt, you know.'

'Maybe,' returned Davy. 'So what you been up to then Ronnie?'

Not long before Ronnie had split from his wife and had been making the most of his new found freedom, as he liked to define his separation. He had left his wife of seventeen years and his son and daughter, although now well into their teens, had taken it badly. He missed his wife, but his natural virility had taken his mind off things. Saturday afternoons were now the beginning of eventful weekends and Ronnie expected that he would not be sleeping alone tonight. He determined that he was headed to Grey's club if all else failed, although a night in the Bigg Market should see to it that this last resort was unnecessary.

Famed for the beauty of its women, Newcastle's Bigg market, and the Groat market below, had recently become a playground for pleasure-seekers far and wide. And not only to drinkers from the North East of England. Since being voted the world's fifth best nightspot by an independent American magazine, and topping even Rio's Copacabana Beach, the Toon had further gained in popularity so that people of all nationalities and races congregated in the undulating square looking down to the castle that gives the city its name.

A little rain would not prevent the hoards of revellers turning out for him. Dressed for the Costa del Sol; fashionable men in tee-shirts and slacks; women in mini-skirts and tops, often little more than sexy lingerie and stilettos, drinkers ensured the reputation of the Toon was well deserved. Many a Sunday morning was accompanied by a crippling hangover and an embarrassed goodbye to a stranger, met briefly before twelve and taxied home to bed. But never Ronnie's.

Ronnie never needed to apologise for anything to anyone. Since his early beginnings in Byker Ronnie had learned that his size and demeanour meant much in The Toon, and he had not felt fear since his first fight in Botto's at the bottom of Shields Road.

'Here. Tell your Harry that's for him. Tell him Jimmy said "Hello."'

The injustice of the back-hander had enraged young Ronnie so much that he came of age that night. After a couple more blows to his face and stomach Ronnie had roused himself ensuring Jimmy could give Harry Carlson the message himself. With Jimmy speaking through a wired jaw and from behind a pair of dark glasses his brother would be eager to listen. Pleased he'd been to wrong foot the bully. With a kick, or rather a leg-breaking back-heel, to Jimmy's shin, his assailant, though able to fend for himself, had been doomed to failure from the outset. To think, Ronnie had not hit anyone for over four years, and then only as a young schoolboy in Bolam Street.

'Not much since the wedding, son. Wor Lass. I'm tryin' to make her see sense, and I'm sure she will. But for the minute, she's havin' none of it. Cannit get her to even speak to us on the phone. The kids are furious with me, like. Cannit blame them either. But you know me. Cannit stop lookin' at the lasses. How's that cousin o' yours? Celia.'

Davy spurted his beer back into the glass, foam streaming from his nose as he recovered from laughter.

'Celia? Oh, I think she'll be down here the night. Always doon here on Saturdays.'

'Aye, Canny lass her. Bonny ain, an' all. Where d'ye think she hangs out?'

Despite the fact that Carlson was almost twice his cousin's age, Davy freely volunteered that Celia would be around the Haymarket and around St James's Park. She'd probably head over to the Mayfair to see a band afterwards. Celia had said Carlson was a looker, and she had been impressed with the charismatic older man's swagger on the dance floor. 'Love a bit o' that,' she'd confided to him at the wedding. Perhaps tonight was her chance, thought Dave.

'You know Davy. Its a shame ye didn't help out with that proposition, when you had the chance. I mean, Tommy, he was keen on the idea. I could see that. What did you reckon? I mean Jerry. He's a bit behind the times these days when it comes to taking good opportunities.'

'Well Ronnie, I don't know. You know Jerry. He likes to

think he's proper respectable. No, not that you're not. I mean, its just not his way. He's never been into gambling. Probably the only vice he hates. But, no, he'd never go for such a gig.'

'Aye, maybe. But from what I hear, he's not going to be in much of a position to turn things like that down forever. Hear he's up to his eyes.'

'Well Ronnie. Howay Man. I'm not gettin' into that. What you having?' He stood and knocked the last of his beer into the back of his throat. 'Ex again?'

From the bar, and it was busy already, Dave turned round and leaned back facing in Carlson's direction. Man of the world, he thought. Carlson was clearly one of those gifted people, for there were women too, who could cross the generational and even gender gap, and were able to talk on the level with anyone. He admired this gift. It was that, amongst all others, that Davy longed to possess, and which he knew, he was well on his way to acquiring.

Chapter 14

'Carlson? He's got a cheek. Who does he think he is?'
Tommy was furious that Davy had been out discussing his affairs, the affairs of his dad, his family, with the slimy Carlson, and felt no compunction about saying so to his brother.
'How could you even drink with the prick? You saw how he goes on with women. Look at Celia, for God's sake. Old enough to be her granddad. What a slimy prick.'
Davy thought of the wedding day, and the chance meeting he had in the pool room with Celia. And his bother. Perhaps Tom was jealous. There could not really be any other rational explanation for Tom's sudden dislike of Ronnie. But he knew better than to bring this fact out into the open, particularly now with Tom in such a mood. In fact, he thought of the way he often suppressed his feelings more than he'd like in connection with a discussions with Tom. Elder brother or not, it was about time he spoke up.
'Listen Tom, I don't know much about that. Perhaps he is just a lucky bloke where women are concerned…'
'Fuck off will you…'
'Hang on a minute, let me finish.'
'Davy, shut it! I Mean it. I won't have any mention of his name round here where I am. That's final.'
Davy tried to reopen the discussion, but it was too late. Tom grabbed his cue and walked from behind the bar, through into the corridor and into the pool room. This

would have to wait. Davy watched as Tom walked briskly over the chequered floor.

'Black and white. Just like the toon,' he thought.

'Ronnie Carlson. Why do I know that name?'

Siobhan had just arrived and was sat in the kitchen while Gill and Davy were preparing the sandwiches for the day. A production line had been formed as usual with Davy spreading margarine and filling onto the bread; tuna, ham or cheese, before Gill stood cutting and packing them. Siobhan joined the end of the line and joined in by placing the cut sandwiches into paper bags, twisting the tops and placing them neatly onto the display box.

'Starting to fit right in now, aren't you?' teased Gill.

Siobhan blushed, but was reassured by both their smiles. She carried on.

'He's been trying to get us involved in a bit of dirty business and Jerry wasn't interested. Now Tommy, who was interested to begin with, has now taken a dislike to the idea – or more likely, a dislike to Ronnie Carlson. Unbelievable!'

'What you saying there Davy? I heard me name.' Tommy poked his head through the kitchen door and scrutinised the trio. All working for the common good.

'Good work there. Well done Siobhan. Getting stuck in, I see.'

Gill and Davy both looked at each other and shrugged surreptitiously, and without even Siobhan's noticing, so happy she was to be doing something right in her brother-in-law's eyes. Difficult, to say the least, the opening up of their relationship.

Tom entered the galley kitchen and squeezed around Gill to stand by the electric kettle.

'Tea or coffee?' looking at Siobhan.

She replied that she would have black coffee. Gill and Davy asked for tea. Tom leaned over between Gill and Siobhan's shoulders and picked up a handful of sandwiches in his left hand, grated cheese spilled onto the stainless Formica surface as he lifted them over to his side.

'Hey! What ye deein' Tom? These are for the customers. Get off, will ye?'

Davy looked directly at his brother.

'You need to get off your arse and help around here Tom. We aren't here for your benefit. Maybe get out of that room and muck in a bit.'

'Management material Davy. Can't be getting me hands dirty on these trifles. I need to be thinking o' bigger things.'

'What? Another pool match, is it?' Gill stared directly. Two against one.

'Oh, I can help a bit more, if you like.'

'See. Siobhan there, she's more than capable. And happy to help, aren't you Siobhan?'

Siobhan reddened at the mocking tones of her brother-in-law. Likeable enough, she supposed, but this wasn't quite right. Before she could stand up to him,

'You need to make more of an effort Tom. I mean it.'

Gill looked at Davy. As staff, it was not her place to tell Tom, but Davy was right. Again, as always.

'Just as well I made you all a drink then. Isn't it?' Tom poured the boiling water into the four cups before handing tea to Gill and Davy.

'How d'ye have it Siobhan?'

He handed her the steaming mug.

'Anyone who drinks black without sugar has my vote.'

Winking as he eased past the three he turned back from

just inside the door. Putting down his mug of black coffee, which read 'BOSS,' he addressed his team.

'Listen. I know things are tough, but we'll get through this soon enough. I'm not sure if the Old Man's going to be too hands-on when he gets back. I mean, we don't know. Hopefully he'll be fine. But assuming he's not, or more likely, he wants to take a back seat. I think we should have a proper discussion over the way forward. Any thoughts?'

Gill looked at Siobhan, and both carried on finishing off the sandwiches. Davy looked up from his blackboard – he was now outlining the limited culinary options, this time using a yellow chalk.

'We need to think about Carlson. I think its worth considering.'

'Fuck that! I told you, I'm not having owt to dae with him.'

'We need to consider everything at the minute. He kna's we're in trouble with the debts mounting. Maybe he can help.'

'Bollocks! We know what he's after. He can sod off.'

Siobhan, though liking both men, wondered at their contrasts. Looking up she said she realised who Carlson was after all.

'He's the guy dancing with Celia at Linda's wedding. That's him, isn't it?'

'Prick! He needs to stay away from me, I can tell you that. I'll end up flattening the bastard.'

Siobhan wondered at the animosity. Why would Tom be so antagonistic towards Carlson?

'Siobhan, its for you.' Gill handed Siobhan the phone, which hung from the wall close to Tom's face. She struggled past Davy and stood close to him and answered.

'Hello. Colin. How are you? Where are you. Oh Alnwick, OK. When you coming back?

Colin said that he had been down to see his dad again, and he was definitely on the mend. He would be back just as soon as he picked up a jumper for Aidan. The boy was fine.'

'OK Colin. Yeah. Yeah....' She looked at Tom, smiling at him, and added 'Give Aidan a kiss from me. I love you.'

Gill and Tom laughed and mocked her. She felt belittled and humiliated but why deny the facts? And she was married, after all.

'We are all family,' she shouted, half suppressing her urge to laugh. She picked up her coffee and sipped the bitter black liquid. She stared into Tom's eyes over the brim.

'You wouldn't be a bit jealous of old Mr Carlson now, would you Tom?'

'What? Me? Jealous of that smarmy prick?' Tom shifted and switched his hands so his right forearm was now wedged firmly along the top of the white door jamb. Siobhan could smell the aftershave mixed in with the muskiness of his armpit, a sweat stain less than a foot from her nose.

'Is that Lynx I can smell Tom?'

Wrong-footed, Tom shifted again before replying:

'I don't know. Must be. I've only put it on and I've already attracted two gorgeous lasses.'

Everyone laughed, and the tense stalemate was broken.

'I'll be in the pool room if you need me.'

Chapter 15

'Come this way, and we'll have a right laugh. Here, this is it.'
The Prom stretched along the Coast, Northward. The spray blew over from the right, from the East, and Siobhan looked over at the clock face. Ten twenty-five. Aidan and Col were at home again, and Siobhan should be feeling guilty. But no, Celia and her were beginning to buzz. The darkness, dotted with coloured spots, punctuated in the distance by the pulse of St Mary's Lighthouse, took on a fuzziness. Siobhan stared ahead and swept the bay, darkness lightening steadily until she felt a growing hum in her head. She swayed before steadying herself on the side of a car, grey and wet beneath her arms.
'Howay Siobhan. Are you feeling that yet, Pet?'
Siobhan felt like vomiting, but realised the pointlessness of that and strove to keep down her saliva, fighting back the drool as it rose and fell within her mouth, just behind her lips.
'I need a drink.'

'Just act like a babe, Babe.'
Pulled along, Siobhan felt her way along the pavement with her feet, and stepped up and along the platform towards the back of the queue, linked into her companion's arm.

'Hello there Ladies. No need to queue. This way.'

Bemused, Siobhan looked down and danced along the Astroturf floor-covering, in through the double doors and up another step into the space ahead. Guided quickly over to the bar, she stood propped up as Celia headed over to the other end. She looked around and again gagged into her fist. Another lucky escape, she swallowed back.

'Here, drink this.'

The women clinked glasses and Siobhan copied her friend as she swilled the fluorescent shot-glass. Bitter and spicy, she swallowed the burning liquid.

'That'll settle yer stomach.'

Alone again, she turned and leaned back on the rail behind and started to focus on the lights in front. Four speakers boomed, each three foot high, and each suspended just below the ceiling in a row above a corresponding row of TV monitors. The strobe light flashed and she stared across and down the step onto the dance-floor. People, beautiful fashion-conscious women, some wearing little more than bikinis, tee-shirted men clad in Chinos or pegged trousers, bounced and jumped around in slow-motion animation. She stared and felt her back twitch, just below the nape. She began to feel a recurrent shiver, as pleasant as it was unexpected. She chewed at nothing and felt her face break increasingly into a broad imbecile smile.

'How's it goin' then? Hitting the spot by the looks of things. This is Dave.'

Siobhan smiled as the red and green lights streamed across the room. Dave, loomed in front of her, his head and shoulder length hair huge in front of her. His flashing smile beamed before he turned, bent and kissed Celia. Siobhan looked on as the pair kissed.

'Enough now Dave.'

Celia broke and handed Siobhan a glass of Coke.

'Black Russian. Lovely. Get it doon ye'. Celia winked and swallowed half the glass.

'We went oot bifore. Doon the Toon. Aye, had a meal in Don Vito's, and a few in the Monkey Bar.'

Dave nodded,

'Its good there, mind. What d'yes have?'

She had linguine Bolognaise. I had the Veal. Best in the Toon. Started off with the pizza garlic bread. Two bottles of red, an' all. Not surprised she's struggling. Aren't you Pet?'

Siobhan, again almost gagging, focused involuntarily on the rising vibration as it travelled smoothly up the top of her spine to the nape of her neck. She shivered, smiled and turned to the bar.

'Ye should ha' seen her Dave. She was coming back from the lavvy and she sees this lass. Well wife, more like. She went ower to her, and I just couldn't believe it. She just stepped in front of 'er and stared reet into her face. Bent ower and stared reet at her. I thought she was ganna smack her. I had to gan ower and grab her. Didn't hear it all, but got the tail end.'

'"Sorry," the wife says. "I really couldn't help it, but rules are rules," ye kna. Siobhan was having none of it. Just says to her; "Who the Hell do ye think ye are, you stupid Cow?" Ay, she said that. Then she picked up the wife's glass and tipped it ower her. The red wine hit her reet in the throat. Poor lass, I felt a bit sorry for her. She stood up and then fell ower. The table went flyin' and there the wife was clutching at her neck as she fell ower. Red wine ivr'ywhere. We'll not be gannin' in there again for a bit.'

'I wouldn't care, but I had just had a row an' all. Some owld bloke at the next table aboot half an hoor bifore. Tried chatting me up. Met him at Linda's wedding. Not a bad looking fella, but you kna' the type. Think they own ye just cos they get a snog. Well I tel't him where to gan, an all. Maybe it was me that started her off. Anyway, we had to get oot o' there sharpish. Left them a big tip, but probably won't cover the mess she left.'

Siobhan swilled another drink as she passed the two shot glasses to Celia and Dave.

'Just tellin' him aboot Carlson and that woman. What a neet Siobhan.'

'She said it was the one that wouldn't let her in to see Jerry when he was in hospital that neet. What a temper she's got. Fightin' Irish, or what!'

'I'm feeling this now. I really am. I've got this vibration going on, up and down my back. What about you Celia?' Dave smiled. Celia giggled and winked at him.

'We'll have a dance, should we? Come on Dave. Come on Pet.'

Chapter 16

Jerry's wheelchair ascended the ramp at the rear of the pub, and the driver steered him through the door and into the lounge.

'Alright Son. Ower there please.'

Jerry pointed to the corner and eased himself out of the chair and into the settle, and behind the Britannia table.

'Get the lad a drink Gill, will you? Pint?'

'No mate, I'm driving. I'll just have a Coke, if that's OK.'

'Aye, get the lad a Coke.'

'Nice place you've got here. I always loved Amble. Lovely room this.'

The driver looked around at the lounge and the newly spruced bar. Gill had spent the morning cleaning all the optics, the shelving beneath the counter and especially the wall and bench on display around the till. The liqueurs formed a three tier pyramidal display for the customers. Drambuie, Galliano, Tia Maria. Adjacent were port, sherry, Spanish red and white wine, the latter's ageing cork protruding in contrast to the unopened red, the green bottle almost half full – or was it half empty, like the bar most days?

'Come and sit down, Son. Just for a minute before you gan.'

The community transport had travelled steadily from Newcastle, dropping off everyone over the three hour sojourn around rural Northumberland from Gosforth and Morpeth, through Rothbury and Widdrington, Alnwick and Alnmouth through to Warkworth and then finally here.

'I'll sit with you for a couple o' minutes, and then I need to be away. Picking a couple up on the way back.'

Gill laid the Coke down and placed a mug of tea beside Jerry.

'What? I'll have a pint Gill. Gasping.'

'Jerry, are you sure?'

'Too right, I'm sure. Haven't had a pint for ower a fortneet. I'll have the Ex.'

Addressing his driver, Jerry pointed out that Scotch was most people's favourite here. He was an Exhibition drinker. Unless he wanted to go for the cask, which he often did.

'You'll not get a better pint anywhere in Northumberland, I can tell ye Son.'

Gill placed the Exhibition, large head settling quickly into the oversized pint glass.

'Thanks Pet.' Jerry picked up the drink and swallowed half the light coloured ale, a white moustache remaining above his lip.

The driver accepted the sandwiches Gill placed before him.

'Aye, well done Pet. The lad needs sommat to eat. Nowt like ham and peas-puddin', eh Son?'

The driver agreed and gorged on the stottie. No need to be over-polite here.

'Anytime you're here pop in Son. You're alwi's welcome. I owe ye a proper drink. Nae bother.'

Jerry relaxed and looked around the bar.

'Anyway Gill. How's ev'rybody been? What aboot Colin and Siobhan. How they gettin' on?'

Chapter 17

'In a minute Beck. I'm just chatting to Seamus here.'
Siobhan watched her mother's face darken and her mouth
tighten. Like the pressure cooker she swore by, if not for
the restraining weight of social embarrassment, her
mother would have blown moments ago. Yet she sat,
motionless. And not for the first time had Siobhan
witnessed this.
Dad always seemed to offer trips out to Dublin on his
return from England. The zoo, museums, the Memorial
Gardens – that was the last ruse. And each time it was the
same. Would today be any different?
All had seemed OK earlier. Off to the train station.
They'd walked through the centre of Carrick, the three of
them happily focused on the road ahead. They had left
the Housing Executive estate, wandered down
Summerhill and along the high street before heading over
the bridge to the station; the mist rising in the early rising
sun. This was in the days before the daily commute to
Dublin. Before the rise, and fall, of the Celtic Tiger. The
platform, when they arrived, was deserted. Another forty
minutes before the train's arrival.
'I knew we should have took the car,' barked her dad.
'We could be half-way there by the time it comes.
Feckin' joke! I mean look at that. Three and a half hours.
It's less than a hundred miles – that's thirty mile an hour.'
He walked across to the timetable board.
'Sligo. What about that? We've a train comin' in a

quarter of an hour. That'll be alright. When was the last time we were there together?'

Beck thought of the last time the visited Sligo. Siobhan had still been breastfeeding when Damien decided they should 'wet the baby's head.' The idea of visiting the city again with her husband, just back from London and with plenty Pound notes in his pocket. It was lovely. Windy streets, old buildings by the harbour. The seaside nearby. But there was little chance of seeing any of that with Damien's thirst. He was always like this. How was he when he was in England?

'You said we were going to see the Book of Kells Damien. Why else would we be going out today?'

'Oh, c'mon Beck. It makes no sense. Waiting all that time and then a three hour ride. Let's go tomorrow. Wc'll take the car. I could do with a nice long drive.'

Damien thought of the long journey from London, through Birmingham, Wales, Anglesey. The wait around for the ferry, unless you were lucky and managed to arrive in time. Nowhere worse than Holyhead, he thought.

'No Damo. We were meant to be going to see the book. It's free to go now. Let's stick by it.'

Siobhan looked on. Wide eyed, she waited for her dad to explode.

'Oh. Alright then,' he relented. 'But I don't see why.'

'C'mon Damien. Damien! Damien? C'mon.'

'We'll get a taxi.'

Siobhan watched as the taxi emerged from under the covered rank of Heuston station and entered the road opposite. Along the bank of the Liffey, over the bridge to Northside, the rain spattered the window outside as traffic wove in and out on either side. The grey embankment wall sped past and she looked down at the black carpeted interior of the floor below her. She felt sick at the stopping and starting – one of the reasons her mother had been keen for her not to journey to Dublin by car. She closed her eyes, feeling the drool amassing in the back of her throat.

I should say, she thought. But she didn't.

'Look mate. It's not a big deal – I'll pay for the clean-up,' said her dad, gagging at the reek coming from the floor below. 'She couldn't help it. How much do you want?'

'It's not just the clean-up. I'm gonna lose a day.'

'What? Its not even four o'clock yet,' replied Damien menacingly. 'How much do you want?'

'Well you're looking fifty. Minimum.'

Damien looked at the Dubliner and reached into his pocket. Pulling out his worn brown bill-fold, he sat back before replying. Steely determination in his eyes.

'Drop us at Conway's first, then we'll see.'

'Give us me money first,' replied the driver.

'Get us to Conway's, then I'll pay.'

The short drive up to the historic North Dublin pub took only a minute.

'Right. There you are, said the Dubliner, hopefully.

'Righto,' rejoined Damien. 'Here's the thirty we owe you.' He handed the money to the driver. Looked at him and added 'Have an enjoyable night off.'

'Come on, let's go,' he said, and looked around at

Siobhan and Beck, waited for them to safely exit the car before looking at the driver and getting out himself.

'Cheers Mate,' he beamed.

'Poor fella. Are you alright Luv?' said Beck, looking at Siobhan.

'She's fine. Aren't you darlin'?'

Damien felt ahead of the game. Power over him, he thought. London had taught him a lot. A man his size was not one to mess with. In spite of his successes on the GAA field, he had not managed to translate that to the streets. Not until England anyway. There. That was the place to be. A man could be a man in England – in London.

Chapter 18

'Billy. Billy Boy. What a name. She used to call her boyfriend that, and he used to get mad.'
'Why should I care?'
The blond shaven head, shining in the sunlight. Rainlight more like. Irish eyes. Smiling. Prod? Brit? What the fuck. Don't care. Love the berry. Beret! Snake badge. Serpent from a viper's nest come to Emerald Isle. Eire! Idiot. Brit.
Accent.
'Scotch, are ye? Aye. Whay aye? How are you?'

> Soldier, Soldier, won't you marry me
> With your musket, fife and drum
> Oh no, Sweet maid, I cannot marry you....

'Tried he's best. Well done. Down again. 16-3:23-1.'
Carrick drizzled on. Again.
Sloppy pass. Sloppy pitch. Grey stand. Amateur ground. Amateur pitch. Mayo. All Ireland. Dublin. Little county. Little club. Hurley.
Slitter smashed forth. Over or under. Up and under. Eddie Waring. Up and under.

Slurrp. Maybe just the one lump. Plop. The lump fell from the tongs and dripped into the mug. Lounge.
Could have a better coffee service. Letting the side down. Mayo. Clifden. Great view.

Dad drove to Ireland's most westerly point.

'The views are tremendous,' he'd promised.

Mist, fog, drizzle. Nothing to see but mist and fog.

'Wanna lift ladies?'

Mammy watched the dripping girls, yellow cagoules wetting the seat next to me.

'Where ye from then?'

'Canberra.'

'Falklands?'

'That's a ship,' one replied. 'Australia. The ship, Falklands hospital ship, named after our capital.'

Always so proud of themselves and Australia. Oz. Who could love a country called Oz? Always dumbing down. Oz. The Church. Siobhan thought of the stage dripping with girls, wet Tee shirts. Boobs out. Blaring music and loud-mouthed cobbers. Paul Hogan.

The Hayward Gallery's Abbo art. Real I am! Not the Aussie Impressionism she'd seen in books.

Who were all these Aussies? Always roaming Leitrim and Dublin. They roamed all over Ireland. Always Irish roots. Were they Irish in Sydney? Or were they Australian? The passports said Australia. Why the pilgrimages?

'We just arrived by ferry on Sunday.'

G'day. G'day.

'She's got relations in Newcastle.'

Billy Boy. Big boy!

Siobhan thought of the Northumberland Fusilier. Young, blond, shy. Her ex. From somewhere in Northumberland, beside Gosforth, Newcastle.

'Northumberlad.' Liked that, he had. Her Northumberlad.

'Keep away from that bastard!!'
Dad spent most of his time in London. Why did he hate him so much?
'You're forbidden from seein' that prick!'
Whatever!
Bundoran. Rides. Rides! Big boy Northumber-lad.

The mug quenched her craving for the dry coffee. Caffeine and syrup from the sugar laced the back of her incisors. She swallowed. Something stirred in her – not the coffee.

Northumber-lad. Just as well he was shy. Bundoran could be rough, but the blond had blended and they walked arm-in-arm. Hardly opened his mouth. Promenading the cliffs and roads below. Madden's Bar. Black and white paint.
'The Toon,' he'd said. 'Guinness. Nowt like hyem.'
Siobhan had felt alive and not for the first time.
Billy Boy, too stupid and shy to talk, cried like a bairn.
'Bairn.' Scotch? She'd comforted the young blond, and had her way. A second hand Granada, PVC seats, swishing wipers and whooshing blower. Foggy windscreen and windows all round. Tape recorder. Wham. George Michael. Elton John.

Wake me up before you Go Go.

The clock chimed again. The bell hovering slowly away into the lounge. Third time lucky.
Granada. Not bad. The bed was better.
Withdrawal. Auntie Mary Margaret had told her all about

it. Hop on. Stay on. Hop off. All good. Don't delay mind. Mary Margaret, sang out the mantra like a joke, laughing at Siobhan's puzzled look.

'You take him in hand, take control. Don't trust the men to give a toss. Have your fun, but don't get caught.'

Mary Margaret smiled and told Siobhan not to mention her little chat to Mam.

'Just between us. And remember. Don't get caught holdin' the baby.'

Good old Mary Margaret. Good Catholic? Siobhan smiled and mounted the supine lad. Forward she leaned, slowly kissing him as he trembled. He hid his eyes in her hair. Her lips reached his neck. Billy gyrating beneath her, faster, sobbing. Cute.

'Ahhhhh,' in union.

They collapsed. Effluent staining. Withdrawal success. Mary Margaret, thanks a lot.

They held each other, clean white cotton sheets beneath the satin-like eider down. Rain smashed against the panes, white light encroaching the dimming grey around the bed. She reached down and wiped his midriff. Crumpling sheets, damp and sticky. Safely gathered, she pulled off the sheet and threw it to the floor.

'Gotta go. Before me Dad gets back.'

'Ma, are you alright? What's the matter? What's wrong?'

Dad didn't return alive to Carrick, but there was plenty of fuss made to ensure he had his return home, as was right and proper. Always said he wished to be planted on home soil when he died. No expense spared. The post mortem, when it came showed he'd had a massive heart attack. It took nearly two weeks before the hospital released his body, and that was the verdict of the coroner. We all knew that.

'Well, we need to bring him home. Can't leave him there where nobody knows him. Cares about him.'

'Ma, he's gone. What difference does it make?'

I realised it was crass, but I was hurt too. My Dad. Gone. At fifty. Forty-nine actually.

Couldn't take it all in and withdrew for a while. Off the rails.

Started smoking and hangin' around the water tower. All sorts of shenanigans. Garda at Ma's door.

He was returned and interred. Gran was distraught. We all were.

Up North. In the North. That was livin'.

Chapter 19

Tom didn't see what Linda saw in her husband.

'Can't fight, cannit fuck and cannit play football!'

He rocketed the ball into the bottom corner and glared behind over his right shoulder. Ian sat there and momentarily caught his gaze before averting his eyes to his wife and sipping his pint. His cue, held vertical in the crook of his knee between his legs, Ian addressed the women sat around the table, all friends of his wife.

Another ball slammed into the back of the pocket, and Tom rushed over to the corner before stooping, eyeing the cue and slowly pushing the ball towards the purple spot ball. It trickled slowly into the middle pocket as the white rolled over into position for the black. He cued the ball and sent the black ricocheting into the bottom corner.

'Rack 'em up Ian.'

Ian turned from the women and stood.

'I'll be with you in a minute ladies. Just got to answer Tom's challenge. Ain't that right Man?'

Stooping, Ian pulled out each ball from the slit and placed them slowly, meticulously on the baize protector and into the triangle. Slowly he rose and pushed the triangle from the cushion, off the rectangular protector and onto the baize arena below. With his cue he led the triangle back to the cushion before gripping it and repeatedly placing it onto the black spot. Tom looked on. Contempt evident from his every glance. He looked sidelong as he sipped from his whiskey and coke.

'Jack and Coke. Pretentious prick!' he thought.

He preferred plain old fashioned Scotch or real Bourbon. Ian could do nothing right in his eyes. Tom watched as his opponent slammed the cue into the rack of balls, each scattering but nothing going down.

'Your shot Tom,' he said, quickly taking his position next to Linda and her friends.

Tom bent to aim as the group laughed, five young women laughing along with that prick. The red spot, three, fell, thudding into the middle pocket as the cue-ball steadily sidled up to the top cushion and onto the blue number two ball. He potted this along the cushion dislodging the yellow stripe obscuring the jaws of the pocket. The cue ball shot off down the table and lined up with the purple. Ian ignored him as Tom glared at the back of his head. Women, thought Tom. He hit the cue ball hard and watched as the purple slammed off the side of the pocket.

'You're on. Ian. It's your go.'

Ian took a long draught of his pint before standing up.

'Back in a minute girls.'

Stepping over to the table he bent and tapped the cue ball. It rested squarely behind the two striped balls, tightly snookering Tom with the two corner cushions behind.

'There y'are Man. Your go.'

Linda and the women laughed as Ian stood by them winking and swigging from his pint.

'Want another Jack 'n' Coke, Son?'

Ian called over to the barman and ordered another round.

'Bring them through will you Marti? I can't leave Tom here.'

The ladies again laughed. Tom bent over the corner of the table deciding on the next shot. Prick! thought Tom as he bent and stretched up the table and played the cue ball slowly off the two corner cushions. The ball slowly travelled down the table missing the erratically clustered assortment of stripes and spots on its way to the far corner and towards the green spotted ball.

'Oh what a shame.' Ian laughed in the women's direction, winked at Linda and looked directly at Tom.

'A miss, I think, Matey.'

The women screamed and Linda scurried away from the spilling drinks as the black and white chequered lino floor was covered in beer, lager and Jack Daniels and Coke. No laughter now as she sat crouched in the corner below the table, her cousin raining slaps and punches on her husband. 'Get off Tom. Get off him you wanker!' she shouted, pulling her cousin by the hair, fists and legs flying in various directions.

In seconds, barely after the fracas had begun, Tom stood and brushed the beer from the bottom of his trousers. Ian stood slowly, cowed and conciliatory, before Tom reached over, grabbed his Riley and poked the butt into the stomach of his opponent. Ian fell back onto the stool, which had luckily been repositioned in time for his fall.

'Don't take the piss! I mean it.'

Tom stormed from the pool room, brushing past Martin, the barman, who almost dropped the tray of drinks as he was barged past.

'You pig! You're a bloody pig!'

Linda followed Tom out of the room, standing just outside its doorway.

'You pig!' she repeated.

Chapter 20

'Well I think he's a better player than you Tom. Yeah, he's been playing in our team and he's captain now.'
'Because they're all crap over there.'
It was a rivalry unspoken but the pub in Holy Island, away from the mainland, the hustle and bustle of Northumberland, and Amble in particular, had a growing reputation on the pool circuit. Last time The Queen's Head had taken on The Ship on its home territory in Amble the Queen's had wiped the floor with the players. Tom, as the Queen's star player and captain, had beaten his two rivals in his two matches. The Ship were lucky to have come in with three games won. Now though, things had been changing.
Linda and Ian, after their wedding, had moved to the island and Ian had become a local celebrity on the pool circuit. While never having been a bad side in the past, The Ship had always lacked the killer instinct when it came to tournament play. After eighteen months with Ian at the helm the team had been transformed into a force to be feared throughout Northumberland and the wider North East. Linda was proud that her husband was a respected player, and revelled winding up her cousin in the Queen's, Tom's home turf.
'Aye Tom. I think you'll now find that he's your match at any table, and I think you are going to find it difficult to beat him like you think you can everybody else. Much improved, I think you'd call him.'

'We can always play dirty like him. He's a prick.'

'That's me husband you're slagging.'

Linda smiled, teasing her cousin. She could see by the way Tom was fidgeting that she was getting to him, and she liked it, as she always had. Not that he was a bad bloke, or anything. But she liked to keep her cousin on a short reign. Best way to treat him. Or he'd just get an even bigger head. Again she smiled as she offered to drive him over to her place for tea. Obviously, as expected, Tom declined, scowling into his coffee cup.

'Oh, come on Cous! You're not scared of a little game between family and friends, are you?'

Tom eyed his cousin. Why was she teasing him like this? She was one of very few who could make him feel pressured, and she knew it. Ever since they were children together, she had chided her cousin and seemingly always got the upper hand. Would she ever leave off? he wondered.

'We've actually got a pool table in the front room. Comes in very handy. And not just for playing pool on.'

Again she grinned, this time directly and brazenly at Tom.

'Very good with his hands Tommy Boy. Much better than you, I can tell you.'

'Fuck this!'

Tom stood up from the Britannia tale, swigged off the last of his coffee and placed the mug with a thump back onto the surface.

'Let's go.' He walked off to the basement.

'Don't forget your stick. You'll need that Cous. You're going to need all the help you can get, I can say.'

'We gave The Ship a towsing last time we played them.'

'You can do better than that Boyo.'

Linda, teasing her cousin again, she knew that he was feeling the pressure. And he was going to feel a lot more of it before they arrived home. She switched on the cassette player.

'Oh I love this.'

> Wake me up before you go-go
> Don't leave me hanging on like a yo-yo
> Wake me up before you go-go....

She twisted the dial, further increasing the volume and the pressure on her cousin.

'Why do you always have that cue with you Tom? Ian, he is great. He's got his own favourite cue but he can play with any. Its a bit like a little comforter, is it, eh?'

Tom looked up and thought of replying but decided to stay quiet. The music boomed.

Muzak, he thought.

'Ian and his team played last week. Five – two. Hammered them! Last time they played – before he was captain – they beat The Ship six - one. Bit of a turn around. Lindisfarne Inn six – Ship one.'

'Oh, Kajagoogoo. Great.' The tape continued unsettling Tom and Linda relished his discomfort. Her car, her tunes. Why was he such a dick when it came to music?

The car swung right, cornering from the A1 and onto the single lane. The causeway was just ahead. About a mile away. They drove onward without speaking.

> Too shy shy. Hush hush…

'Like the music Tom?'

Approaching the causeway Linda slowly braked and the

car trundled to a halt. She turned to look at her cousin and pointedly glared into his face. Their eyes met, and they both connected again. Tom leaned across and placed his left hand on Linda's thigh – searching for the top of her burgundy knitted tights before his hand was slapped roughly away. She leaned in and slapped a peck on his cheek, coaxing him and promising with her gestures a resurrection of their past playtimes. He leaned over but missed her mouth and landed a peck on the black hair, just above her left ear.

Just as he thought, Ian was a prick. He stretched out his left arm and attempted to grab her right shoulder. The car door opened and Linda escaped. In her left hand she held the Riley. Tom's special cue.

'Oh, let's see. What's in here then? What a lovely purse you've got here Tom.'

She unzipped the case as Tom chased her over, catching his jumper on the handbrake and ripping it as he scrambled over the driver's seat in pursuit.

'Ooh, what a lovely big long cue. Lovely. An' you certainly know how to use it, don't you, Cousin? Let's have a better look, should we?'

Tom grabbed and lunged at his cousin desperately attempting to wrest the cue from her. She danced and sidestepped away from him heading swiftly into the dunes, car door open and Tom rushing to exit the vehicle before she got too far.

Oh Vienna…

Tom stumbled and his teeth hit the ground. Broke, the left incisor was smashed and blood dripped from his mouth as he rose from the concrete. He picked himself off the ground, knees bloody and left hand grazed. Above him Linda turned and looked down on him. Shocked to see him bloodied, but resolute, she dropped the vinyl case and began screwing the pieces together. The cue, full length, emerged from her breast. She held it aloft and faced the North Sea.

'Linda! Please. Give us it back. Please.'

Holding the cue at its tip, Linda bent her arm behind her as if to use its butt as a club. She hurled it with all her strength and the cue hurtled forward and down the dune whipping and twirling through the air before smashing against a rock emerging just above the surface of the water.

'No!' shouted her cousin.

Barging past her, Tom stumbled and staggered upwards and down through the marram grass towards the sea. Toward the beach below them. Towards the shattered Riley, which floated in three pieces in the breakers of the gently approaching tide below. Its tipped end drifting, its turquoise chalk staining the surf, highlighting the wound. Blood from his lower lip dripped into the water, approaching the cue. He picked up the pieces, and the tip, so delicately cared for and conditioned over hours of honing, dropped into the sea.

'You bastard Tom. You bastard.'

The engine revved and from the corner of his eye Tom saw the car head over to the island. He knew this was a blow that was going to take some getting over, and dropped onto hands and knees into the shallow sun-swept water as Linda, once his lover, now his assailant, sped towards her husband. Further and further away from him.

Chapter 21

The fire roared in the grate, coals and embers licking the air – fiery tongues against the black back. Dragon's teeth before the opening.

Billy looked down at the liquid in the glass. A pint of froth – or so it seemed. The beer had never been that great here, but now things seemed worse than ever. The barman, a stocky ginger youth watched as Billy lifted the poker, prodded, poked and sat back. The poker replaced with a clatter on the hearth below.

The yard called him forth – the hooter sounding in the lunchtime sun.

He walked down the lane, under the railway arch and saw the glare before him. The Tyne stretching towards the shore opposite in a round sweep. Dust wafted in his eyes – the right stinging, he rubbed it and lifted his hankie to push away the grit. Wind blasted against his face. His eyes, both of them, watered, a tear streaming towards his lip – sunlight rain.

Ahead the boiler suit, navy and booted in black, bobbed towards the works. Better stay back. Not much to say. No words to convey his fear of the yard.

The head, bounced like a football. Step, down to step, beyond into the murky water below. A dry dock, it was called. But seldom were they dry entirely. An amalgam of Tyne and rain. Pooled below as the pandemonium rose.

'Hoo Man. Get oot the way. Grab the Gib! Git the chain!'
The gantry crane above slowly swept overhead, gib, swinging loosely from its chains, was grabbed and held by the pole. Tamed for a moment, the ganger looked downward and noticed the head below. Bouncing no more. Settling into the pool, blood seeping as it mixed with the river and rain. Brain fluid.

Joe was one of the lucky ones.
'Gan an' get yer coat Joe. You're wanted ower in Hebburn.'
The Hebburn Yard, which worked interchangeably with Walker, accessed by ferry, was a miserable cousin. Inaccessible before the Slake – Joe moaned about his tea getting cold, the kids in bed. Such was the inconvenience. He was happy in Walker. In the boiler by day – mornin' 'til neet, but home by dinner. Noo Hebburn. What a bastard!
By the time he arrived they were both gone. John and Trev, marras for weeks, dinner in the Ellison and Raglan, a walk doon Pottery Bank and up the plank, into the ship's hold. They'd suffocated as the air was replaced by carbon monoxide – CO2- no that was carbon dioxide. CO.
A week off and Joe was back again. In the same boiler. Two new marras.

The grate cracked as the fire hurled sparks up the chimney. Billy swallowed as he tipped the foaming liquid back into his open mouth, down his gullet. Two gulps, eyes wide, he dropped the glass onto the Formica top.
Over to the bar, the lad behind the bar stood up and turned from the crate of tonic bottles. Yellow on grey

vinyl floor.

'Same again Bill?'

'No Son. Gi's a Broon Ale.'

The barman twisted round and grabbed the pint bottle below, across the floor. Reaching back, he placed it on the towelling mat. The top fell beside it as he dropped the opener, to be caught by the string.

'Pint or half?'

'Pint.'

Billy handed the pound note, and the coins – correct money – and turned back towards his table next to the fire.

'Fuckin' warm!'

Broon, or as some called it, Dog, was never Billy's beer of choice. But he'd never been one for lager. The beer here, keg Ex, was undrinkable.

Joe drained the schooner and opened another bottle, before replacing the empty back into the red crate – a trademark in itself. Joe liked always to have his own crate as he pursued his marathon session.

'Naebody can drink a crate in a session!' So many time's he'd heard it.

Joe proudly swilled the fizzy liquid, almost black and white, like the Toon, into his gob. He topped up and the fizz foamed in the rounded glass – half pint wine glass without a stem.

'Aye Son. You did well gettin' oot o' there. Too dangerous!'

'Mind them ladders, mind. Divn't wanna risk it on them windaes just before you're off.'

Billy had started a round of window cleaning just until his papers came through. A couple of weeks. Then off to pastures new. Wherever that was. He expected it would be Germany, although things were said to be bad in Northern Ireland. Better there than ower in Germany, mind.

Joe agreed. He still hated the Krauts. Never set foot in the country. Never would! He remembered, and reminded his nephew of, the horrors of the camp. Dickies, fleas.

'We saved them up in matchboxes and threw them on the guards.'

They had been treated fairly well, but Nana and Granddad, and Dad and Auntie Florence, thought he was dead long ago. Not a word. Not like in *Colditz Story* anyway.

'At least we weren't Jews. Or Gypsies. Or Russian.'

Joe always felt himself lucky to have been British, despite the inequality of the Depression. The war had only enhanced his logic; not least because of his knowledge of the treatment of prisoners. The Germans, where he was anyway, were a least pretty humane. But the Japs. Fuck!

'A mate o' mine, Pete, was in Burma. Used to give he's stuff away before gannin' back from leave. Knew chances of comin' back. When he was brought back from the Japs he was a skeleton. Disgrace! Nae apologies or nowt! The Jarmins were tried. Not the Japs though. Scot free Hirohito.'

The beam swept the room – a torchlight shone in a cavern. The barman lifted the hatch, walked out and approached Billy. Lifting the empty pint glasses, he placed them on the stool top below, lifted the bottle and wiped the cloth around the Formica top in swirling motions round and round hoping Billy would lift his beer.

He replaced the bottle, lifted the pint, half full of Brown Ale, and scoured beneath.

'Gis another will you Wayne? I'll come ower noo.'

'Hope that foghorn stays off the neet. Sick of it.' The beam reappeared and lit the room.

She didn't seem like the others mind. Not so mad as them Northern twats. You couldn't be sure though. Didn't seem common like the ones in Belfast. Or Londonderry – Derry? Whatever. What a way to gan on.

The streets were like middens. Couldn't fathom why people would gan on like that. Ower such a shit-hole. Women sittin' in doorways. On doorsteps with a fire on the pavement. Well, smoke, anyway. What a mess. What a view.

Kids. Rocks and bottles iv'rywhere. Abuse everywhere. Why? Why had he volunteered for it?

Fear had ruled his Walker days – what might be below deck. Fear still ruled him. Cowardice? he wondered.

No, he was nae coward. But he had a dull constant feeling. Always present. Whatever the weather. Whatever the circumstance. He could not get rid of the feeling of unease. Aye, some of he's mates were lappin' it all up. Some of the hatred, especially that Essex bloke. But Billy didn't think all these people could be bad.

Terry and Sabrina. They were from Ireland. Used to give him he's ball back. Alwi's smiling. Sweets alwi's handed oot. Specially on Sa'days. When Terry came back from the bar. Me Dad knew Terry well. Great mates.

Here though. Naebody had owt to say to you but callin'. Brit scum! Cunt! Bastard! Go home! Was this not the UK? What a shocker.

You'd never trust those bitches. Those snaky little bitches. A good fuckin' then a good slap. They're all the same, Billy thought.

'Hold the line, there lads! Hold it! Don't let them scare you.'

A rock, lifted from the terrace wall and hurled, full pelt, landed and struck Robby as it bounced. Full in the face.

Why the fuck weren't we wearing helmets? thought Billy, as another missile flew past, his comrade's boots disappearing from view as he was dragged away and mounted onto a stretcher.

'Ye Cunt! Cunt!' The blonde, hair clinging to her face, sweat and spit dripping from her face as she spat the words.

'Me?' thought Billy. He looked along the line of troops beside him. The mayhem ahead.

'You'll be heading into bandit country. Those of you that are new to this – this is it. Don't let them get under your skin. Remember, these are the UK's worst civilian populations. And there's no room for sentiment.'

'Slam!!' The rifle, turned backwards so the butt faced the crowd, stopped abruptly as it hit the blonde. Blood spurted from her mooth as she fell to the floor. Billy looked at the teeth in front of her. The crowd seemed to be invigorated. More so now. It surged forward. Bodies fell – not like dominoes, more higgledy piggledy – random topplers.

The jeep, like a battleship becalmed in front on the

asphalt sea ahead, crowd in between, suddenly moved forwards. A three-point turn parted the mob before whirring through the rank – his rank.

'Back! Back to the truck.' the sarge was yelling.

Bodies continued to fall as butts shot out towards the crowd. 'Ginger bastard!'

Billy's face froze. Spit ran down into his mouth. Bloody spit mingled with his own. He gobbed back to the boy ahead and turned. He backed towards the open lorry. Jabbing, stabbing and shouting.

'Back! Back!'

An arm lifted him aboard and threw him down onto the bench. He regained composure. Troops thrown beside him. Away. The tail gate raised as the lorry quoined the corner.

'Welcome to The Emerald Isle!'

The Cockney; lance corporal Briggs, punched his shoulder.

'Cunts!'

Billy had fought enough on Shields Road, Raby Street and The Bigg Market. This was something else though.

'Why did I come here?'

'You've been here almost six months now Flynn. How are you settling in?

Major Worlmsley, serving his third tour of Northern Ireland, was always seen as approachable and liked the men, in his way. Obviously, things were different here, on UK soil, as they say, than back home. The likelihood that they would run into one another in civvies, let alone have any sort of relationship, was slim. Worlmsley came from farming stock and would be returning to the farm when this was all over. At any rate he'd be resigning his commission in a couple of years anyway.

'Settlin' in fine, Sir.'

'Yes, Flynn. I can see that. You're making quite a name for yourself.'

Billy had already been promoted to Lance Corporal, and it was evident to all around that he was NCO material. At every test he had shown mettle enough to impress. Mentioned in dispatches on one occasion when he rescued three of his platoon from heavy fire in Armagh.

The lass looked good, mind. Nae denying it. Trim figure. Bairn an' all.

Billy stuffed the bread and patty into his mouth and licked the sauce from his fingers and thumb. The crumpled paper dropped onto the tray and he sipped the steaming tea. As he looked up, casting his eyes through the plate glass, GAA posts atop the hedgerow ahead, flagpoles without welcome, he thought of the women he'd known over here.

Colleens. They were called colleens. Not like the girl he

went to school with. Sweaty and sticky. The Irish colleens were rough. And ready. He smirked.

'Can't trust them. Never trust them.'

That Bobby was a prick alright.

He had been patrolling. Again. As usual. Always patrollin'. Never endin'. Then he was relaxed. Christmas. Amazing. Hatred. Name calling. She came ower, offered we all cup a tea. Freezin'. Bobby, as usual, 'Fuck her. No way!'

I took the cup. She smiled.

'Happy Christmas.'

Three of us were led into the newly fitted kitchen. 'Nice!' Modern, aubergine. Smooth surfaces. Ma's hoose was good, I thought. But this scullery was summick else. We stood just inside the patio doors. Boots black, and not from polish, dripping on the lass's floor. The three of us stared roond. Unbelievable.

'Have a piece of Christmas cake Lads.'

The lass was swarthy. Good looking but some age. Not Mrs Robinson. But she seemed friendly.

'We need to be off.'

'No Bobby. Corporal's a bit jittery Missus.'

I stepped over the wooden blocks, kids' coloured playthings, and thought of the irony. Building blocks. In northern Ireland. They all want to blow things up. The chair, orange plastic, very chic, un-comfy, better than nowt. I plonked me arse doon and grabbed the slice of cake.

'Can I use your toilet, please?'

The corporal disappeared as the lady topped-up me cup.

'Seen you around here. Where you from?' she asked.

She had actually been to Newcastle. Visited the Toon. Couldn't believe it. Her da' was a reporter and he used to travel with the paper. Watched Linfield play a friendly at St James's. Loved the place and said she wanted to go back.

What a beauty, he remembered. Black hair. Eyes. Skin like ivory. Bobby always described their skin like that. Complexion.

Oot the next mornin'. In with a chance I could feel it. She approached doon the pavement. I held me breath and handed her me Newcastle pennant. The cloth and tassels hung from the scroll, Super Mac and John Tudor pictured on the inside. As she opened it she smiled.

'No!' She passed it back.

'Christmas is ower,' she said. The laddie by her side, howldin' onto the pram's chrome handle, blinked. She walked away.

That neet we lost two lads. We shot one o' them.

'Coming up for leave, aren't we Flynn?' stated the Major.

'Aye. But I wanna come back afterwards Sir.'

Sergeant Swanson beamed at the Major, who smiled at both his subordinates.

'That's the spirit Man.'

'On your return, we have a little something lined up for you and a few of the other men. It'll be strictly between us for now. Keep it within the regiment.'

Flynn smiled, reddening sightly around the green collar.

'Anything special Sir?'

'All in good time. Have your leave first and then we'll discuss things in more detail on your return. Are you off back to Newcastle?'

'Aye. I am Sir. A week's leave then back again.'

'Have a blast then. Dismissed.'

Lance Corporal Billy Flynn saluted ostentatiously, and in accordance with the Sergeant's orders about turned and marched out the open door.'

Later, sat on the lavvy, Flynn thought over his position. What luck. Here less than a year, and already being seconded. He'd heard that was the way to make a name for yourself. Alright, so far he'd done alright. But noo, the sky's the limit. Flynn had worried that he may be getting transferred to another unit, or worse, a different tour. But all had turned oot as he'd hoped.

Chapter 22

'Look at that Son.'

The stone, a good flat one, skimmed repeatedly over the grey surface before ducking beneath an on- coming breaker. The waves lapped slowly, gently across the estuary beach. Marram opposite. Cross on the mound above.

'I used to swim across here in the Summer when I was little Aidan.'

'Swim?'

'Yeah. I used to swim a lot then. Not now though. Too cold.'

Aidan hurled a rock, flat but too large to carry, even from his lower aspect. Plop! The pebble clumped into the two inch deep wave as it chased the boy's welly.

A cobble, moored alongside a motor launch lay sideward on its keel. 'Canvas tarp ready to shelter its skipper. Or not,' thought Colin. 'Better the launch.'

Bleaching, the sun slowly scorched the estuary. He ran towards the ferry point and turned into the mooring. It was moored on the other side of the Aln. Never that busy, the ferryman must have knocked off early – an irregular service in a remote English village. Colin had to see Davy in the Schooner garden at five. Wind swept the waves out as the Aln slowly retreated back into the North Sea. Somewhat choppy, but hardly wild horses, Col dived into the water beneath.

Surfacing from the flop, he stretched out his arms, one by one in a swift crawl to the other mooring. Blurred murk below, sky and waves at his side, he breathed. Panting within a minute, he paused and treaded the waves. The estuary, the marram topped hillock and its cross all shone above the waves, golden gleam and grey between. The targeted mooring lost from sight. Panicking, the boy drifted further toward the horizon, crawling, scrabbling, kicking across the current. The estuary, shining beacon dimmed as he tired and coughed. Below the surface. Above. Below.

'Come here Lad!'

Colin rose from the water. His side caught the cobble side, the gunwale speared his pelvis as his head, crumpled beneath his neck and shoulder, landed on the wet deck. Blood spewed into the pool of brine, and the skipper threw him head first beneath the covered bow.

'What ye thinkin' Son? What ye daein'?'

Colin coughed and vomited. Seawater puke stained the side of the bow.

He sobbed and cried. Where was Davy?

'Never go swimming by yourself Son. Daddy was a silly lad and I nearly drowned.

'Drowned?'

Aidan fell to the beach as he ran from the water's edge. Covered in sea, he screamed. Col grabbed him and hugged the dripping lad.

Siobhan was always surprised by the scenery. A short walk away the tracks led to London. The East Coast Main Line, a principle route in England heading North to

Scotland's capital and beyond. London to Edinburgh. Flyover. That's what they called it in America. Somewhere so backward so as to be unworthy of note. Had she not met her husband, she would never have visited such a place. Yet here she was. Again. Often cold, rainy. Wind-swept. But always interesting.

Aidan played halfway down the hill below. Grass halfway to his chest. Coarse sharp dune grass seemed to carry the boy further away. She climbed upward as the boy grew distant.

The morning sun glinted into her eyes and she squinted as she reached the summit. Below, Aidan scrambled towards her and grasped and tugged at the long grass.

'Come on Aidan! That's it!'

Encouraged, face contorted, the little curly head bobbed up and down amid the grass. He approached. Siobhan surveyed the estuary below. The Aln, once meandering behind her feet had changed course overnight, she'd heard. Tempestuous history, just like the county, and the North generally. Just like home, in a way.

St Cuthbert, once atop the hill here, hardly a remnant now. Cut off from the town. Alnmouth had been a successful Nineteenth Century port, good links to the surrounding neighbourhood. Fishing and trade. First the cross of Cuthbert. His Church. All cut off from the land across the river. Stream, more like. Then the town, as it must have been. Slow growth in size before the ancient centre. Then the slow decline. East Coast Main Line – far from helping the town – or village? - strangled with goods from afar.

Aidan grabbed his mother's calf, biting her ankle above the grass.

'Ow!! You little...'

Laughing, the young woman lifted him and hugged him to her bosom. Perched, cheek-to-cheek, they surveyed the beach ahead.

'Drowned. Daddy drowned.'

'No. Daddy's OK. He's in the hotel. Don't worry. Daddy loves Aidan. Doesn't he?'

Siobhan kissed his cheek. Put him down and headed to the cross in front, on the summit. Grey tablet below:

CUTHBERT
684 AD

The place seemed desolate now. Here and over there.

Chapter 23

'Ye see Siobhan, an age in astrology is about two an' a half thousand years, and each is the age of the Zodiac. You've heard of the Age of Aquarius, right? Well that's what they're on aboot, ye kna? Every twenty six hundred years, if I remember, or however lang, I can't remember exactly, we're pointed at another star sign. Well, constellation, I mean. Like the Plough. That's a constellation. Ye see?'

'To make things harder, the ages are divided up into another twelve eras – aye, they're also the Zodiac – like Aries in Aquarius, or Taurus in Sagittarius.

'What you saying Celia? Do you believe all this then? Are you really into the telling the future, astrology. All that kind of stuff?'

'Well I'm not absolutely sure Siobhan. But even if I'm not, it makes nae odds. Gotta remember. The people who've made the decisions in history, they were believin' it. The Romans made sacrifices and consulted the burnt offerin's. The Bible gans on aboot Abraham sacrificin' he's son. These are the leaders and they believed it. So all the famous things in history then were decided after the local magician or priest, whatever you wanna call him, or her sometimes, whenever they had took their readin's.'

'But it's all superstition and mumbo jumbo, isn't it?'

'Aye, it might well be, astrology and fortune telling. But remember, the' all used to gan and see the oracles an' priests. What d'ye think they are daein'? Making sacrifices, readin' the stars. Battles and big decisions happened on the basis of all this mumbo jumbo, as you call it.'

'Anyway that's how it went then, definitely. I'm pretty sure the eras are a hundred an' eighty years. Not a hundred percent though. On top o' that the eras are divided into phases.'

'I think they're called phases, anyway. Mebe aeons, or something. Not sure. I could show you, I have a book aboot it.'

'These are all just fifteen years lang. Aye definitely. And to complicate things, the ages, eras and phases all rotate in the opposite direction, all in relation to your stars. Like spirallin' in different directions.'

Seems a bit complicated, and maybe a bit far-fetched Celia.'

The older woman took a drink from the table and took a couple of sips before returning it to the table. Celia continued.

'I mean, I bet ye didn't kna that the Sun, and wor solar system, rotates roond the Milky Way. That's wor galaxy, an' that takes millions o' years to fully rotate – it gans reet round the centre of the galaxy. Its called a galactic year. But let's not get into that. We'll be here all neet, eh?'

'Anyway, the Ancients, whoever they were, have knan this. Certain groups, whether they're obvious to us, like the American Indians, some tribes in South America, as well as other groups, like new agers, have plotted this forever. Oh aye, the Egyptians, wi' the Pyramids. Them an' all.'

'The question is; are there still groups o' people who follow this? It's called esoteric knowledge, and people are still bang into it, believe me. Do you think the astrologers in the papers, like Mystic Meg or Russell Grant, d'ye think they're makin' it up, like?'

'Aye, ye dae. Well they divn't. They're not makin' it up. Whether they're good at predictin' mind. That's another story.'

Celia leaned forward and grabbed the drink, took a long draught and ordered another round.

'So you say that world history was decided like the throw of a dice or a look at the stars, then Celia?'

'Aye. It was. Certain it was in them days. Noo? Well I'm not sure. But there's plenty of evidence that people are still making big decisions on the stars, and stuff.'

'Oh come off it Ce. You're not serious, are you?'

Celia leaned forward and looked Siobhan in the eyes.

'All I'm sayin' is this. Ye, or me, we divn't have to believe in it. But if the leaders of the world dae, then that's canny important. And loads o' people say they dae.'

'Look at the start o' the forst world war. That was started in Yugoslavia when a group o' Freemasons killed the prince of Austria. Frank Ferdinand.'

'Franz Ferdinand. It was Franz.'

'Anyway when that happened the stars were all in place and Sirius, the Dog Star – sometimes called Isis– it was lined up with Orion's belt.'

'There's more to it than that, and the book'll tell ye.'

'An' then when the killers were tried after the war the stars were aligned again. It had all been arranged.'

'Siobhan couldn't believe that Celia was thinking all this.

'Takes all sorts,' she thought, listening to the sing-song accent and marvelling at her companion's drunken enthusiasm.

'An' did ye kna that the car that Prince Frank died in, al'reet Franz, it predicted the day of the end of the war?

11,11,11.'

Siobhan smiled, stifling a laugh. Hardly able to keep her eyes open, she relaxed back into her seat, listening to her new friend's weird ideas.

'Anyway, I'm getting' off me thread noo Siobhan.'

'We're not in the Age of Aquarius, and that's what people think. We're noo in the Age of Pisces and in the Era o' Pisces. The supposed date of Jesus's birth. One AD, that was the beginning of Pisces. It'll end in the middle of the twenty-second century. But, ye see, there are big changes comin' and that always happens as the age gets on. There'll be plenty of upheaval. You watch. And it'll all be good. Gotta be positive, Man.'

'We are actually in the phase of Taurus, noo. The bull. Just left Aries. That was a hard phase. If you look ye'll see how things have been gettin' better lately. Look at when I was little. Thatcher, The Miners' Strike, Ireland and the IRA. It's nae accident that things have been settlin'. Look at Northern Ireland noo. You can also see South America, Mandela and Apartheid.'

'An' things are ganna get even better. Upheaval, aye. But for the better. Good times are on the way Siobhan. I'm tellin' you? We're heading towards Aquarius, and it's ganna really be amazin' then. And I kna that's not for another hundred and fifty years. But we'll feel the effects for a lang time afore that.'

'Look at all the ages back. Ye can see a pattern. Its called End-time. No, not the religious fanatical shite. This is written in the stars.'

'It's just coincidence though Celia. I mean there are loads of conflicting things going on all the time Celia. Both good and bad – positive and negative. Look at the news. It's easy to pick things out to make your argument.

Doesn't mean you're right though, does it?'

Celia took a breath and looked up from the fireplace and directly at Siobhan.

'Listen. Ye had age o' Cancer. It was nearly ten thoosand years ago. That marked the end of hunter gatherin'. People settled doon into toons an' cities. They started livin' in hooses. That's Neolithic.'

'Then they went into Gemini. Ye see? It moves on just like in the Zodiac signs ye see in the papers. Same way. Anyway, Gemini lasted for two and a half thoosand years til aboot six thousand years ago. That's when they started exploring past their little communities, and they spread roond the Mediterranean and the Seven Seas.'

'Ye kna, Sinbad and the Greek myths. Ulysses. That was all from aroond then. Sinbad the Sailor, ye kna? Well Ulysses, the Roman sailor, is the same gadge. He is also the same Greek myth, an' all. I forget he's name, but they're all the same stories from the same time, all moved aroond as the people moved aroond.'

'Well, I don't know,' replied Siobhan.

She began to turn pale and put her hand over her mouth.

'Oh, I am really feeling that.' She sat back and relaxed trying not to vomit.

'The Seven Seas were all round the Middle East. That's when the first civilisation came alang. Sumer. Then Babylon. That's all roond the time o' the flood. Noah's Ark. Adam and Eve and the Garden of Eden. The Devil as a snake. Moses and the Ten Commandments. Its all real, but written doon and messed around, and writers misunderstood the languages of the Bible. Real, all based on fact.'

'Just like the Greek and Roman myths, they all come from the same thing. All from these tablets the Sumerians had. Ye've heard o' the Good Sumaritans? I think that's them. They're from Iran aboot ten thoosand year ago. And they gan on aboot some aliens that created us, and fought among their sel's. They are the cause o' the flood, and for destroyin' Babylon. All this is written doon on these baked clay stones discovered last century. They are the original Bible stories and the ancient myths.'

Siobhan looked up and laughed.

'Come on Celia. What a load o' rubbish. Aliens! Rubbish!'

'Well, I dunno Siobhan. Is it any different in believin' in the Bible stories as they are? Not sayin' I dae believe it, like.'

'Oh! I'm absolutely fucked! Really am. A'm ganna get a taxi. Can ye phone 'us a taxi, Pet? Will ye Siobhan? Come back to mine an' I'll show ye what I'm on aboot. The books a've got at hyem. Ye'll see what I'm on aboot.'

'I think she's a bit of a tit. That's what I think. All the new age crap. She should focus herself a bit more on reality, and then she might make something of herself.'

'Oh, come on Col! She has a good way with people. Just needs pointing in the right direction, that's all. I mean, conversation. She can go on and on. And on some more.'

'Yep. That's Celia. Always been like that. Ye know she had Tommy wrapped around her little finger. He was besotted by her, or so I heard. Not that he seems to be missing her now, though. Moved on, I suppose.'

'So what is it about then?'

'I spoke to me dad. He is thinking of taking a back seat with everything. Not before time. Not quite retiring' yet though. He said he doesn't want the others to take over. He's asked us if we'd be interested in running things. He says he knows I'm not that interested. I haven't spent all that time at college to be a barman. But he knows you 'd thought about running a pub back home. He asked if we could take it on and you front the whole thing. He'll let you know when we get there later.'

'What do you think? Interested?'

'Well I have just been helping out really. Like anybody would. What d'you think Col?'

'Don't see why not. If you fancy it. I mean, we've got nothing keeping us in Ireland have we? Been here for nearly three months and not missing it? Are you?

'Well, I like being there, but no. Not really. I also love it here.'

'So he's wanting' me to take over. How come? I can't understand it.'

'He's wanting us to take over Siobhan. But you'll be the one doing it really. I haven't got the time, nor the inclination. I'm not gonna get involved, I doubt. But we'll see.'

Chapter 24

'Seventy Eight.'
'Eighty five.'
'One hundred.'
'Go on Harry! Well done.'
Harry's mate shouted encouragingly, as Harry stepped up to the oche. The bar, crowded with drinkers was also hosting the charity darts competition, a special event to raise funds for the local cardiology unit. Funds had been steadily dripping to the bigger cities at the expense of the local hospital in Morpeth, which often saw patients being rushed to either Edinburgh or Newcastle in life threatening situations.
'Seventy-two.'
In all, the tournament saw a dozen teams from the region compete for the trophy, one especially donated by Frank Armstrong, the organiser and local Morpeth businessman. Armstrong, who described himself as an iron monger and hardware man, and had other interests on the side, epitomised a local pillar of the community and helped many people less fortunate than himself, ensuring many were able to get a leg-up early on, to ensure they had the start in life he'd been denied.
The cardiology unit was in dire need of funding, nothing proved that more than the recent incident when his good pal Jerry Compton suffered a heart attack. Shaken, as Jerry obviously was, Frank felt things may have been different for him, as well as countless others, had there

been a better facility locally. This darts tournament was one of a raft of measures he was planning. Through the local Freemasons, of which he was a leading member, and through his connections as a Rotarian, he planned, as usual, to change things for the better.

'Seventy-seven.'

'Good to see you Jerry. Nice to see so many people here tonight. You could say that they're all here because of you. In your honour, so to speak.'

'Well, aye. You could say that. But they're all here because of ye Frank. Aren't they?'

'Let us not dwell on the niceties, eh? Its enough that we are all here. That's the main thing. Now what can I get you Jerry?'

'Guinness. I'll have a Guinness please Frank.'

'And what about you young lady? We haven't been introduced. I'm Frank. Frank Armstrong. Siobhan, isn't it?'

'Nice to meet you Mr Armstrong. I'll have a Guinness too please.'

'Frank. Call me Frank.'

'Julie, two pints o' Guinness and I'll have a double. Make it Glenfidich this time, can you?'

'Ninety-eight.'

'I've got Bill and Geordie coming. They're taking part in the tournament. Ower there. Should be finished in a half hour or so.'

Jerry and Frank laughed.

Siobhan saw that there was a lot happening here that she was not party to, although this was why Jerry had brought her along. She smiled politely as Frank corralled her over to his table with his free hand. He sipped from his glass with the other, finished it and indicated to Julie with a wink to follow the three of them over with the round.

He sat with his back to the bar, straddling a leather upholstered stool, and motioned to them both to sit at the corner booth. The pair of them settled into the leather upholstery as Julie placed the tray of drinks before them. She served the Guinness, placing them on the cardboard drip trays advertising Newcastle Brown Ale. She then placed Frank's malt whisky in front of him, then placed the jug of water by it's side. 'Clooney Whiskey,' it read, yellowed and mottled all over with a network of hairline cracks.

'Look at that. Shamrocks an' all. In honour of our guest from across the Irish Sea. You are honoured. Well done Julie.'

Julie smiled at the two guests and backed away, smiling throughout her retreat.

'One hundred and forty.' Spectators cheered.

'You know Jerry. It is times like this when we see who our friends really are, don't you think? I mean look at all these people. Mostly friends of yours. Mutual friends. We are all very lucky.'

Jerry nodded and smiled at his two companions.

'One hundred and eighty,' roared the compere, his voice trailing off as the spectators cheered.

Siobhan looked around at the bar. Four men were sitting playing dominoes bordering a polished square tray. Shuffling, one of the old men, leaning across the tray, dropped ash from his roll-up onto the tiles.

'Whoa Man. Watch it! You dorty bastard. Look a' that.'

'A'reet Jack. Hould on. Nae harm done.'

The shuffler parted the tiles, picked up a cardboard beer mat and scooped the ash on from the middle of the tray and flicked it onto the floor. He blew the remaining ash into the air. Jack began coughing loudly, placing his clenched hand in front of his protruding tongue as his eyes watered.

'Fuckin' Hell Man! What ye daein'? Careful!'

'Give ower, will ye's? Just put yer money in.'

Jack finalised the shuffle and all three put two pence each on the corner of the table next to the shuffler. Siobhan watched as they resumed their game then turned back to join in Jerry and Frank's conversation.

'Ye're not going to tell me, Jerry, that you can't help us out with this. I mean, all the mates you have. Surely some o' them'll be interested.'

'I'm not saying that Frank. But howay, we've got to be sensible. All this could cause a massive stink, and we divn't want people gettin' the wrang idea. You've been roond the block lang enough to kna' that. People divn't like cheaters. An' that's that.'

'Cheaters, aye. But this is only tampering with the odds, even then, only once in a while. Come on, Jerry.'

'Aye, well, maybe. But you kna' what I think. I don't like it. But I suppose, mebe, things are changin' roond here.'

'Yes, Exactly.'

'Here's Geordie and Bill. Hello Lads. Sit down. What you havin'?'

Frank motioned to Julie to come over and replenish the drinks, encircling the glasses just above with his index finger pointing down, drawing an invisible halo around and above them.

'Get Geordie and Bill a pint an' all.'

'Fuckin' useless! Couldn't get into it the neet. Al' reet Jerry. Who's this?'

This is Jerry's daughter-in-law. Siobhan.

Geordie and Bill smiled and greeted her then sat down.

Geordie squeezing next to her and Bill, taking a stool next to Frank. The drinks arrived and they both swilled beer, Bill gulping a few times before exhaling loudly. 'Lovely Frank. Cheers everyone.'

'Jerry and I have just been discussing the situation at Brough Park. We think we can come to some arrangement. Isn't that right Jerry?'

'As I said, Frank. I am not keen on taking chances. But I'm willing to go with the majority. What do you think lads?'

Geordie, finishing off the last of his beer in a long slow draught, placed the empty glass back on the table, turned to the bar and shouted.

'Whoa. Julie. Can ye' get us all another Pet?'

He turned, looked directly at Siobhan and smilcd. IIe then looked at Jerry.

'Jerry, I think ye' kna that things are in need o' changin'. Business has been slow for all o' we. Well I say we should gan alang wi' this. We can dae wi' all the help we can get financially. An' I'm not the ownly one, mind.'

'Ye're reet,' added Bill. 'I need a boost to keep afloat. Really strugglin'. I think Frank's idea might get we oot o' this little hole. A lifeline. Just when we need it.'

'Come on now. Best of order.' The scorer announced the commencement of another match. ' Sixty-eight.'

Siobhan got up and walked over to the bar. She looked behind through the glass fronted refrigerator. 'Can we have the same again please? No, I'll have a Carlsberg please. Would you like a drink?'

'Thanks a lot Pet. I'll have a half o' Scotch. I'll have it later. Don't worry, they're on Frank. Sit down. I'll bring them ower.'

Siobhan, disappointed at the opportunity to take a break

from the men's company turned and headed back to her seat.

'Cheers Pet.'

Bill swigged off the last of his pint and banged the empty glass onto the table.

Siobhan sat down again and waited for the drinks to arrive, self-conscious and cut off from the conversation, as it revolved around the four older men. Discussing things beyond her. Centre forward, outside right, play-maker. Double top, treble twenty, double sixteen. Lamborghini, Ferrari, Aston Martin. Occasionally, normality would return and she would understand enough to input her thoughts, but only occasionally. Introductions to new men, none of whom she felt connected with, except the Cockney – actually a man from Brighton. He seemed to fit in well with the men, although he was able to condescend and talk to her of things she felt comfortable with. Would she ever fit in here? Fit in with all these people? Hopefully, her dealings with them would be limited.

Her head swum and she looked around at the laughing faces, listened to the clack of dominoes, the shouts of the compère as he intermittently announced the match winners, each time punctuated like clockwork the regular stream of seemingly random numbers; fifty-seven, ninety-six; one hundred. Occasionally he reached one hundred and twenty, forty, and twice even one hundred and eighty. With each he sung them to the obvious enjoyment of the cheering group watching, all other drinkers either indifferent or long-suffering of the din at the other end of the lounge room.

Dicky Jameson, regular winner, lifted the trophy. She watched as the compère introduced Frank and as he handed Dick, Dicky, the cheque. Everyone cheered as he faltered through his acceptance speech and stuffed the cheque into the charity whip-round glass.

It had been a smashing night, and Morpeth, and all those in the area, would be the winners.

She watched as Jerry stood and hugged Geordie. Anyone would have thought they were family. Everyone was happy, and Siobhan gladly took Jerry's coat as they smiled and strolled to the front door.

'Good night Jerry. All sorted?'

'You wanna watch Frank Armstrong, Pet. Wasn't sure until noo, but believe me. He's behind all this. Watch him. And anyone working for him. Don't trust them. 'Cos they won't be your friend, nae matter how they may seem.'

Jerry opened the waiting saloon outside and bent into the front seat beside the driver.

'Al' reet Hinny? Yer in? We wanna gan to the Queen's Heed in Amble please, Son.'

Chapter 25

'Mary. Mary. Come on now. Arms in the air, high as you can. That's it. Robert, ye an' all. Come on. Up. Stretch....'
The sea beckoned, as it always had. Beneath the picture window, below the garden stretching forth, the sea beckoned. Grey, flecked with interminable dark specks, topped here and there with the occasional spray of white foam. Foaming from beneath a grey sky, clouds rushing by.
Behind the glass, sheltered from its elements, Jerry looked out. Always out, amid the din of others. Always noise. Never-ending racket as he stared out from behind the glass. Bordered by flowered Laura Ashley, the municipal version; mustards and beige specked with red and blue washed flowers. The glass behind which Jerry now sat, daily, endlessly, offered comfort, and it was this that repulsed Jerry more than everything. Everything. A new life away from the sea. Away from the pub. His playgrounds no more. Swapped for the comfort of the busy day room. Routinely resisting the imposed routine. Medication. Tea or coffee. Breakfast, lunch, dinner and supper. These were the days known to Jerry now. Imposed by family. Loving. Careful. Caring and deliberate. Nothing but the best.
He shifted slowly and painfully reeled, his feet comfortably encased in thick winter woollen socks inside comfortable brown tartan slippers. Rubber soles skidding slowly over the patterned carpet beneath. The sea

beckoned.

Jerry focused as a gull appeared, hanging in the blustering sky. White headed gull – now in its winter coat and devoid of the chocolate coloured black. Black spot behind black eye the only trace of the colourful summer just enjoyed. Swept and hurled on the sea's wind, back and forwards towards the glass then out again over the cliff face and towards the waves below. Back and forwards. Back and forth, left and right, upwards and down. The pull of the pane's attraction too strong to escape, the gull stretched out its red webbed feet and landed two metres from Jerry. They both eyed each other from their respective safety. The bird looked in as it paced round and back on the sill outside. Jerry sat and moved his head. Left and right. Tracing the movement of the bird outside.

'Bastards! Just shoo him away man. Whack him with that knife shank.'

'What? You're kiddin' aren't you Jerry?'

'Just do it! He's gettin ' all the bait, man.'

Arthur grabbed the knife and hurled it over the deck purposely missing the bird. As it left the foredeck he rushed over and gathered up the top of the large bag; woven polythene sheets encasing the slimy stinking assortment of guts and scaly titbits, bloody and wet. An octopus was sprawled dead just below the surface of the pile, pink suckered tentacles curled round a starfish. A dead crab disappeared as he drew the string around the top of the sack and wound it repeatedly.

'That should hold it Jerry,' he said.

Arthur feared the bigger man, or rather feared his disapproval. Never had the older man hurt or even threatened him, but they had something. Arthur feared being cast out of his mentor and friend's side, and was always eager to please.

Jerry looked away and to the sea, away from the Farnes and forward they bounded, waves splashed and settled on the foredeck as Arthur returned, past the mast, beneath the boom and over to his friend. The motor chugged evenly.

'Great day to be oot, mind Jerry.'

'Aye.'

Jerry focused ahead and spoke gently to his young friend. 'Nowt like a good day's fishin' with a line.'

Prancing and marching, head swivelling and bobbing, the gull eyed the old man. Despite the drizzle, which seemed to pepper every view every day, Jerry viewed the gull, its red eye staring back, and through. His only preoccupation to allow escape from this day-room, its activities and fellow residents and staff.

'Granddad,' uttered Aidan, laughing as he climbed over his lap and up onto his left shoulder.

'Big lovely Man. You are a big lovely Man.'

Jerry saw his reflection and thought of the boy's gripping hands, the strong grasp onto his neck. Shouting into his ear.

'Good boy Aidan.'

He pulled the boy down and turned him around. 'Give us a love, Son.' He pulled the boy's cheek close to his own and they hugged close. The boy smelled of Siobhan

'Breastfeeding!'

'That's all we had Siobhan. Nowt else in my day.'

'Yeah, nothing much back then.' Siobhan joked and they laughed together.

The boy pulled away, reconnected his cheek to his granddad before pulling away again, this time climbing down onto the floor beneath. He dropped down onto his knees and looked down at the hard floor. He rubbed at a stain on the lino.

'Aidan! You don't want to be grabbing the floor son. Come here.'

Bending down to grab the child, he lunged playfully and the boy darted away behind his mother. Laughing. They all laughed.

'What you been doing then Siobhan?'

The pub was beginning to pick up a bit, and Siobhan notified her father-in-law that takings were almost respectable. Every Spring the pub game saw a rise in trade and this year things were little different in that respect. The difference was in the way Siobhan had begun managing the affairs of the Queen's Head. Back in Ireland, the mantra was always new management, new staff. Siobhan had been true to this and all but Gillian and Davy were no longer within the safety net offered by the Queen's Head's employment.

'Seems like you're making a go of it anyway. Thought you knew nowt aboot the bar trade. Just shows.'

Siobhan knew a fair amount, and hours from the other side of the bar, in the Angel in Carrick, or from a stool in Madden's on her regular trips to Bundoran, had taught her a lot more than the basics. Long had she sussed that visiting a new place, whether on holiday or on business, necessitated a visit to the local bar. By befriending the locals, particularly the bar staff and management, could a fair impression be made of any place, its nightlife in particular. Lost count had she of the amount of bars she had frequented over the years, whether back home in Ireland as a youngster, or later in life in Dublin and then London. Newcastle, more recently, had become known to her due to her experience of hitting the bars, albeit in company with her new friend Celia.

'I spent a lot of time in front of the bar Jerry. Clearly it's paying off.'

'There's more to it than that Luv.'

Jerry flicked a beermat over the room and through the door into the corridor. As the square boomeranged its way, arcing towards the floor, Aidan ran over into the corridor before retrieving it.

'Well done Son. Again?'

The boy raced back to retrieve the mat again.

'So what has been happening with the staff then? Where's Martin? Where's Tommy?'

'Look Jerry, we need to have that meeting with them. I'm not saying they're hopeless. No. But the business is too family oriented.'

Before Jerry could argue, and he knew she was right, Siobhan lifted a piece of A4 from her laptop bag.

'Look, I have a few ideas here and think we should take a look together. If I am going to turn things around here we need to take a radical approach. We need to bring in people who are not already connected. It undermines me. People are too used to taking us for granted Jerry.'

'Come on Siobhan. Its not that bad.'

As the boy returned once more and then raced off again in pursuit of the cardboard mat, Siobhan outlined her strategy.

'There are times when all this pub was was a glorified boys' club. A pool club in actual fact.'

Her Leitrim drawl sung in sharp contract to the clipped rapid Northumbrian tones of the Old Man. Seemingly ignorant of the family connection that led her into her current position, though undoubtedly very aware, the young Irish mother had moved swiftly into position at the helm of the family business and determined to steer the tiller in a professional direction.

'Things are changing around here Jerry, and we're making a fresh start.'

She handed the old man the paper and he glanced at it.

The prow of the cobble headed north, parallel to the coast and toward Scotland. Jerry had increasingly taken the boat out on his return from hospital and this time was going to enjoy his time with Aidan. The boy, not used to coastal waters and fishing, was enthusiastic and marvelled at each novel sighting – pretty much everything.

'Granddad's going to take you fishing today son, so behave.'

Granddad didn't look at the world that way, the boy knew. Their's was a special understanding. He could do anything and Granddad would be there. That he knew.

'Look Granddad. Land.'

'My little pirate,' said Jerry.

As the helm moved to port, ever so gently, the cobble changed course, ever so slightly. Now the boat was sailing towards the far side of Longstone.

'Granddad. There they are.' Aidan pointed.

Bobbing, up and down with the waves, often submerged, the focus of the boy's attention was obvious to his granddad. Whilst far from novel, Jerry could now appreciate the sight through new eyes. So often had he sailed this stretch of water. So often the grey seals, famous to the area as one of the world's most important colonies, had bobbed up and down. Never had Jerry watched them with such relish as he did now. The boy, dangerously dancing along the boat's port side, was instilling a new perspective into these animals.

'Oh, Granddad. Granddad, there's one. Look.'

Jerry watched. Not the animals without, but the boy within. Had he been like that in his day. Obviously, yes. But the freshness of the outlook of this lad brightened the day. Retirement suited him, and Jerry was enjoying this moment, like so many of recent days.

'Oh they're great. They're great.'

'Don't touch them!'

Jerry realised that, though he was advising the boy for his own safety, if Aidan disregarded it, nothing would be done in consequence. The sail caught, the boat accelerated, and Jerry felt so close to his boy. Never had he been able to connect like this.

Jerry, the strong man, the hard man, now the frail man, was able to let things go. And how he loved the feeling. To be free at last. Money. Of all the years he worried about the lack of it – and this had been the general tenet of Jerry's life – what could he show for it? What was there that was tangible? The bar. Yes. He had held onto the pub, the business – despite the troubles and the downturn. But all those years worrying about what he now saw as 'the Downturn.'

Gone were the days when Jerry could hold the attention of a packed room full of patrons. Before the Strike, when money was splashed around liberally, Jerry had known that all was well, and that he made the right decision in becoming a publican. Yeah, this was an occupation, amongst many other interests. But it took up much of his time in the Seventies when he was preoccupied with entertaining his customers and the community. Then, things had been easy, or so he found later.

But what followed....

Jerry thought of the good times. Jerry thought of Valerie. Val. Jerry thought of the later years.

Not knowing how he had arrived in his present position, at the helm of the boat with a grandson he hardly knew, he headed the boat forward. Aidan looked around again and staggered back towards the old man.

'I love you Granddad, love you.'

Less than a year ago the boy had never met me. Jerry loved the boy, curly headed and smiling up at him, or pointing to the seals, or grabbing the anchor – which he had forbidden, again and again – or just climbing over his knees to interfere with his control of the helm.

'What's that?'

Jerry looked behind him. The boy pointed and laughed as a porpoise fell below the surface again.

'A porpoise Aidan. Like a little dolphin.'

Aidan grabbed the helm, wrestling his granddad, but not really. Aidan knew he couldn't win a fight, and he enjoyed playing like this. The boat was Granddad's, but Aidan was in charge. Today he was in control of him. And Granddad loved being with him. He could get away with this. He pulled the stick from Jerry's hand and pulled hard.

'You little bugger. Get off!'

Aidan dropped the tiller and ran toward the front. Ducking beneath the sail, he goaded Jerry. Jerry steadied the boat and looked at Aidan.

'No. Leave it.'

Aidan grabbed the anchor. Again.

'Stop it Son. I mean it. Good boy. Put that down!'

The boy dropped the anchor back under the tarp that made up the only shelter from the elements.

'Its alright Aidan. Come here! It's alright.'

Aidan sat on Jerry's knee. They both stared out and over to the island.

'Look Son, there's a gannet.'

Jerry pointed as the bird glided overhead and took aim at the surf below. The bird folded its wings back and bombed below the surface'

'Where's it gone?'

Aidan searched but the bird was nowhere. He soon looked away and pointed again at the seals laying on the rocks. Closer, two heads bobbed. The boy, new to the sight of the seals, pointed again and again as the heads approached.

'If you're good Aidan, they might come over to us.'

Jerry pointed to the anchor that Aidan had just thrown beneath the tarp.

'Be careful Son. Pass me the anchor. Pass it over here. Don't throw it.'

The boy again scrambled along the boat's deck until he reached the bow and stooped to pick up the anchor. Returning, he held it out in both hands struggling with its weight.

'Only ever do this when I am watching you. Be careful. Go on throw it over the side. Face the bow, the front, and keep away from the rope.'

The orange nylon rope followed the anchor swiftly to the bottom.

'How deep is it?'

'Its about a hundred feet Son.'

'Can I touch the bottom?'

'You could never touch the bottom Aidan. Its three times the height of our roof.'

Aidan clambered back onto his Granddad's knee and looked at the seal, now less than fifteen feet from the side of the boat. They both stared at the animal as it watched them.

'Let's have some bait, should we?'

'Bait?'

Aidan, still unused to his granddad's colloquialisms as well as his accent, wondered what he was getting at.

'Pass me that box ower. We'll have some bait. Share some with yer friend here, eh?'

Jerry opened the Tupperware and pulled out half a stottie filled with ham and butter.

'Do ye want some stottie cake?'

Jerry saw the confusion in the boy's eyes.

'Cake? Where?' He looked into the box.

'Stottie cake Aidan. Here.'

Smiling, Jerry ripped the half into two quarters and handed the boy the ham sandwich.

'This is stottie cake Aidan. Its breed. Bread, I mean, Son.'

'Soda farl. Its a farl Granddad.'

Aidan took the sandwich and watched his granddad move his towards his mouth. Synchronising, the boy bit. Both stared at each other. Aidan clambered back onto his knee as Jerry tossed a lump of stottie into the sea. They watched as the seal lunged and grabbed the sandwich in its jaws. 'Wouldn't like a bite off him,' said Jerry. 'Look at the teeth. Sharper than a dog's.'

They both stared out into the North Sea, the boat

undulating amid the swell. Shuggie in motion as the seal's head vanished and reappeared as the boat bobbed.

'Its getting rough Son. Look at the clouds over there. Black as neet. I mean night. Best be gettin' back, I think.'

'Oh, Granddad.'

Tacking starboard, the cobble slowly but steadily stalked the shore as the seals and Longstone grew distant, its lighthouse, red and white hooped, a distant conning tower above the rock. The swell grew, rising and falling, up and down. This was no challenge for Jerry though.

'Nae bother here Son.'

Aidan snuggled into his granddad as the boat headed back towards Amble.

'Don't worry. I've got biscuits as well.'

He handed the boy a couple of bourbon creams.

'You can have a dash when we get back.'

'A dash?' Aidan stared up at his granddad.

'I'm forgetting you're a foreigner Son. I mean you can have a shandy. You can have some real beer an' I'll have one an' all'

'I cannit even read me own writing here.'

Everyone laughed and Jerry regained his authority by shouting down his son before taking a long draught from the coffee cup. Sweet and creamy, the old man looked piercingly at everyone and quiet ensued.

'As I said, I'm off to Alnwick in a bit. Ye can come alang Davy. We need to pick up a few kegs.'

'I'm sticking the rota up behind the bar. Make sure you all take a look at it, and be sure to follow it. I'm sick of the lack o' cleanliness of this place. Look at it.'

The staff avoided Jerry's eyes as Martin and Gill smiled

back at him.

'We need to get some mixers and soft drinks an' all Jerry.'

'Aye, Martin. It's all in hand. We'll head off in a bit.

'Look Dad, we need to make sure there's enough food in for the pool team the morrow. We're playing The Viking, and there'll be a big crowd. We've got the darts team playing on Wednesday, an' all.'

'Aye, Tom Son. I kna that. But we need to really be thinking aboot makin' sure we've got iv'rything.'

'Have we got enough pies and sausage rolls Gill?' asked Tom.

Gillian glanced at Tommy before looking back at Jerry and addressing him and Martin, her colleague.

'We seem to be short on wine and there isn't enough Stella. We had to put Carlsberg through the Stella last neet Jerry, didn't we Marty?'

Martin looked at Tom before verifying that they had ran out of their premium best seller on the previous night. He added that they were also a bit short on Wild Turkey. Tom flicked a torn beermat over the floor.

'We need to make sure we've got enough of iv'rything in Man. Don't run out again!'

'We need to take control of the pub Jerry.'

Siobhan pointed her finger at points on the list, the paper laid out flat in front of her father-in-law, upside down from her perspective and readable from his.

'This is the main thing Jerry. We need new bar staff. We need to phase out your kids and get in proper staff.'

Jerry agreed, though reluctantly, that the ship needed to be tightened, and that a steadier hand might be in order.

'Look. Just see the way Tom was drinking. He was

drinking whenever he wanted and never paying the tabs he'd racked up. Nothing but the best either. Malts, Jim Beam. Wild Turkey. Why do we have three Bourbons here anyway? Who else drinks it?'

'Aye, Siobhan, I never said he was great for the profits, but I like having Tom around. Brought in plenty of laughs.'

'Well, he may have done once, but that stopped when he was endlessly treating the place as his own pool club. His mates. His rules. His pub. That's how he thought of it Jerry.'

'Aye, maybe he wasn't the best with the money side of things.'

'Look Jerry. Fine. He's your son and we're not here to slag him. But let's just start fresh. He's off to Spain now. He's making a fresh start. Why can't we? Come on Jerry.'

'Just a minute Gill? Give us a minute or two, can you?'

Gillian, the barmaid stepped back through the doorway as her new boss asked. Although it was getting on, and the pub needed opening in twenty minutes, she busied herself in the kitchen. Aidan followed her.

Jerry longed to leave the bay. Surrounded by glass. Cocooned within the carpeted windowed outward-looking enclave, staring at the birds and longing for the open sea, or the pub cellar, his inner sanctum, his own sanctuary. Here he sat exposed and open to all. Unable to hide away, manipulated hourly by well-meaning nurses or care staff. Often less than well meaning.

Jerry was almost constantly and patiently persuaded to drink up, sit up or turn round. The daily exercise class, better than sitting doing nothing, he knew, but boycotted. A principled protest waning towards acceptance. The sea beckoned.

He looked out as the rain gushed onto the path ahead. Leading to the cliff edge, out to the North Sea, Jerry looked ahead, the wind-swept greenery of the garden, the gazebo to the left, cloven by the asphalt and bordered by the fenced off cliff edge. Beyond, the sea beckoned.

Fishing, trawling with his cobble. Managing the bar. Laughing, joking and idling away the time with friends, his family and the custom. Arthur. His long-time friend – side kick, some had said. Ahead the sea beckoned.

Sandra bent over and pulled. Her right hand between the top of his arm and his left breast, not quite in his armpit. His side ached in response.

'You need to sit up Jerry! Come on! Sit up! This is no good. You know that.'

The young woman. Twenty five? Strong as an ox, and manipulating her patient.

'You're the last to drink your tea Jerry. Hurry up!'

Sandra. Swept back brunette, clipped back hair between a lengthy fringe, freckled and pale, glanced at her wrist watch. The shift was over ten minutes ago. Supposedly.

'Jerry, I've told you before. Drink up! I've got better things to do than wait around 'til you decide.'

Sandra rearranged the cushions behind Jerry. Waif-like, she towered over the once powerful old gentleman as he sat his ground, cowering inwardly at the girl ahead. Fronting up, he hoped she'd leave him to his thoughts.

'I said 'Move!' Come on. I'm not telling you again Jerry!'

Jerry leaned forward and to his right as the girl again searched behind and beneath him. An unhealthy clinical unenduring intimacy. He reddened.

Jerry retired to the privacy of his room at seven-fifty pm;

as soon as the communal dinner was over. He liked to sit by himself pondering the day's events and generally reminiscing. Nostalgia, not what it used to be. Jerry chuckled to himself.

He thought of the rose tinted glasses everyone seemed to wear, those he surely wore.

Arthur – great man. The best. Settled in nicely. Always welcome.

Settle. Funny one that. The pub used to have them in those days. Now though. Britannia. Rule Britannia. Ha Ha!

Fifty pence piece. Great coin. Seven sided and silver. The times spent coontin' those. Times changed. And the hands across the sea. EEC.

Jerry had always been interested in coins and had a board with various countries' coins displayed in an assortment behind a glass. He had always intended to make them in to a table, but it looked as though that was now unlikely.

He thought of the coin from the Eighteenth Century. One of his favourites, it was a George III penny.

Look after the pennies, and the pounds will look after themselves. Mr Micawber. Dickens – Old Mr Dickens. Pennies? Virtually worthless now, plenty value to Dickens though. Inflation.

Maggie. Inflation at fifteen per cent, and rising. Only a few weeks at that, mind. Scary times.

He thought of the inflation, and the Tories. If only the inflation had been the problem.

Arthur, arrived late Seventies, now he must be hitting he's sixties. Always a good help. Aroond the bar, in the cellar. Great lad Arthur. Naebody better.

Bay City Rollers. What shite!

Abba. They were the ones from the Seventies. *Waterloo.*

Money, Money, Money.

Siobhan seemed to kna how to manage mind. Nae money worries there. Must give her a ring. See how they're gettin' on. Nae flies on hor.

Lord of the Flies. Noo there's a book. Load a laddies on a desert island. Stranded. Not like roond here, mind. Plenty hot and nae chance of rescue. Or seemed like it. What a shame! The little fat lad. Piggy. Horrible name. Kids. Cruel little bastards!

He thought of the boy's glasses. How Jack and his mob stole the lad's glasses. How he couldn't see withoot them. Didn't care though. Ralph, the big lad didn't help him. The' killed him. Big boulder on the heed. What a shame. Bloody poor laddie.

Far fetched, the endin' mind. All crying togither. Bet they'd get away with it Scot-free. Wonder what would ha' happened?

The black and white film. Not as good as the book. Naewhere near.

Aye, times are alwi's changing. Colour telly noo. Day time telly. Channel Four. Da, Da, Da Da. Great big four. Middle of the screen for oors with that tune. Loved the tune then. Exciting. Couldn't get the advertisements. Had to play the lang tune wi' the test card. Then *Coontdoon.* Paul Coyle, Scotch lad before Richard Whiteley.

Silly bugger. Ferrets on the telly. Hilarious. 'Just playin'. Too right! Harry Dewing got the end of his finger bitten off by his polecat.

'Divn't bite the hand that feeds you,' I said.

'He's gettin' me rabbits though,' he said back.

Fair enough. He loved that polecat. Had it on a lead. Like a dog. Stunk the place oot. Had to get him to leave it ootside.

Jerry reached over to the bedside cabinet and pulled out his scarf.

I'll gan oot the morrow. Into the garden. Divn't care what the weather's like. Unless its rainin'. Could sit in the gazebo.

'Sandra? Oh. I hope she's off.'

Jerry recalled as best he could the day, but was unable to ascertain whether it was now Wednesday, Friday or Saturday.

Definitely not Saturday. Nae football. Always football on the telly.

Berwick Rangers. The local team. But Newcastle. The Toon. Berwick's a little side. Hardly a club at all, really. Only 20 miles away, but playing in the Scottish League. And hardly in that. Second Division. Bottom. Newcastle's the team. Always was. Not changing noo.

Jackie Milborn. Wor Jackie. Best Centre Forward ever played on grass.

Cloughie, mind. He was some player. Had to hand it to the Mackems on that one. They knew a striker when they'd seen one.

Great manager an' all. The best manager never to lead England. He would have won the World Cup. Ron Greenwood. What a joke!

Cloughie was too good for the FA. Wouldn't lie doon like a lap-dog. And Revie. That bastard. Beat by Zaire. Went to manage Saudi Arabia. For God's sake.

What aboot Jackie Charlton. Did well wi' Newcastle. Brought in Keegan. Had to gan then, mind. Off t' Ireland. Beat England. Should o' been England Manager. Just like Cloughie though. Nee shite taken. Great fisherman. World cup winner. Great Northumbrian. Great drinker. Great bloke.

Pity aboot Souness and Dalglish, mind. Never really lived up to the expectations. Never did nowt with the Toon. Probably still helping oot the Scousers. Keegan though. What a man.

Wacker Dixon. Another great bloke. Best trawler-man I ever met. Wouldn't expect a Liverpool man to be much of a fisherman. Grew up in Hull though. Went to sea at fou'teen. What a sailor he was. He's mate went down without a trace back in the late Seventies. What a shame. Wacker really cut up by that. Couldn't fathom it.

Six feet to a fathom.

Anyway, never got ower it. Said he'd started with Arthur, both left school on the Friday and were at sea on the Sunday. Funny way of life that. Never being at hyem. Always away, ten days, fortncct, or whatever. He said it was a tough life. Tough lad. Big lad. Never lost the Scouse accent. Torned oot it was submarines, they reckoned. Pullin' the trawlers doon.

Davy Jones' Locker. Ugh. Wattery grave!

Lassies. He could charm them alright with that accent of his. Had them falling ower him. Never withoot a lassie.

Wonder what Carlson's up tae? There's another one. Philanderer, that's what they call it. Nympho – nymphomaniac. Is that women?

Davy's a good 'un. He....

'Jerry, time for your meds..'

Chapter 26

I've always done me best. Can-nit believe it. Oot! Out!
Dave sat in front of the TV and flicked the remote
control. *Brookside*. Great. He laid the Brown Ale can on
the coffee table and settled back into the draylon
Chesterfield.
Should ha'e got that three seater. Knew it would fit. Too
late noo.
That little bastard. I should ha' waited and asked to leave.
Some sales-lad though, I suppose. Dave rubbed the knapp
of the draylon. Just like velvet. Poor man's velvet, they
say. Good enough for the likes o' me.
'I'll have a pint of that strong German lager.'
What? As if. That's obviously Holsten on draught. Good
beer that. Nae advertisin' on Channel Four. Nae product
placement, anyway. S'pose its a good thing.
Jerry should ha' kept Holsten. Better than Castlemaine.
Aussie piss. Four XXXX. Well called. Good marketin'
though. Ev'rybody was sayin' it for a while.
Well sprung floor technique, as we say in Blyth. Classic
take on the Audi ad. Naebody really had Audis before
that, mind. Couldn't get away with it. The Sierra. That
was my favourite. Liked that more than me Granada
even.
That Sheila Grant. She's a bit of al'reet. Definitely. As if
she'd be gannin' oot wi' that prick.
'Knob head', as them Scousers keep on sayin'.
Good actor mind. Was in '*Boys From the Black Stuff.*

'SDP,' he said. Bella Seaton, oot of *When The Boat Comes In*, she told him. Too reet. SDP!

That's not cowld inuff. Should ha' left it in a bit langer. In the freezer.

He laid the Brown Ale back down and shifted forward, about to head over to the fridge. Fuck it. It'll be cowld inuff when I drink the next one.

Oh, here's Jimmy. Go on son! Ye tell him. Barry Grant. What a prick. Knob 'ed! Aye. Go on son!

Them closes are weird mind. Couldn't fancy a garden like that. No. I like me own garden. When I can be arsed, like. I need to get oot and dae a bit o' weedin'. Hate it though. Really dae. I'll cut the grass the morrow. Aye. That'll be a good start. Should ha got that Qualcast, mind. That Flymo. Doesn't pick the grass up. Pain in the arse. Could dae wi' one o' them rakes. The big fans. Divun't rip up the grass. That one knacks it all up. Rips all the grass oot.

Bad that heroin, mind. Barry's reet there. Aye, Barry, you're reet there, at least. Ye should niver ha' took it in the first place. Then you wouldn't be in this mess, would ye? Imagine? Ya poor mother and father. Bobby and Sheila. Salt o' the earth.

Damon, an' all. Had he's own spin off. He went off wi' that lassie. Bonnie lassie an' all. Poor lad got stabbed, an all. Great piece o' drama. Soap bubble. That was it. What they called it.

Ahhh! Cannit beat a good Broon Ale. Mebe I'll get a glass for it. Aye. The adverts are on noo.

Not lang since, there were nae adverts, eh. Channel Fower. Interlude. Used to be a black 'n' white pottery wheel. In the owld days. BBC. Aunty Beeb.

He poured a new can into the half pint glass, ensuring the liquid fizzed sufficiently to dissipate some of its gassiness. He swigged and poured the rest of the can into the top of the foaming beer. Should ha' went to Mullah's. Hate canned Broon.

Amber Ale. Me grandda' used to mix that wi' Broon. Never tried it. Same bottle, blue label instead o' Broon. Piss, they reckon. Might o' mixed well wi' Broon though.

Wonder what Tommy's up tae? Bet he's off wi' some lass. Some señorita. Coupe of señoritas, likely. alwi's did dae all reet wi' lasses.

The door bell rang.

'Who the Hell can that be at this time?'

Chapter 27

'Eeh, isn't it awful?'

Ellen kissed Colin on the cheek, and he stood back.

'You're looking great Ellen. As always.'

'Well, I'm not sure about that Son. It takes longer and longer to get this presentable anyway, I can tell ye.'

The laughter, strange under the circumstances, was welcome. They both smiled at each other and Ellen touched the young man on his elbow before rubbing it softly, smiling and moving into the chapel. The drizzle fell steadily through the bright Tyneside sunset.

'Come on. Here it is.'

Colin joined the queue of mourners walking to the approaching hearse.

'Alright gentlemen. We'll be right behind you to help if needed, but just lift him onto your shoulder and wait. I'll tell you when, and move slowly into the door, as I say.'

The Chief mourner, the undertaker, directed and the six men followed.

'That's it. Now lift. Slowly, that's it.'

'OK. Everyone OK?'

All assented and he proceeded to lead them towards the awaiting doorway.

'This way gentlemen.'

Three further undertakers escorted the group, and ten men slowly bore the coffin into the chapel. Plastic handles adorned the sides of the casket. As Colin arrived at the appointed place, he joined his companions in sliding the coffin onto the awaiting platform. As he set the box onto the awaiting rails, his sleeve caught the handle. The chief mourner bent and collected the handle as it bounced on the polished concrete floor. It was attached without much notice to the collected mourners.

Colin walked over to his wife, and Aidan grabbed his father by the hand. A hand was placed gently on his shoulder from behind. He politely glanced around and smiled at Julia and her husband in the row behind. He also smiled at Rose before turning back to face the lectern in front, just to the left of the coffin. Siobhan held his other hand as he turned, but he shook it off politely so he could get the notepaper from the inside pocket of his black jacket.

'I have been asked to speak on behalf of Jerry's close relatives, and will be conducting this Humanist ceremony in line with Jerry's wishes. He was not a religious man, although we all agree that anyone who wishes to say a silent prayer for him at the end of the eulogy will be given the opportunity.'

'What about the beer though?'

'Get Tommy to take care of it. Come down here and have a look at this. Here.'

'What is it? What?'

'This is a shirt my dad wore. When he played for Wallsend Celtic. Centre Forward. Best position. Striker.'

'Yeah Granddad. I know what the centre forward is. Not stupid. Played outside right.'

'Well, when he played for them, they were just a tiny local side. Not many professionals there then. Mostly amateurs. At best, semi-pro. He used to make enough money from a day's football to equal his dad's pitman's wages for a week.'

'How good was he then? Second division?'

'Well they sent a scout up for him from Blackburn Rovers. Said he played a stinker and they took Sammy Walsh. He scored the winner in the FA Cup Final. Me dad was supposed to be a better player.'

'He was aboot to be signed for Middlesbrough. They took him to the pub to sign him up. All arranged. He's dad, my granddad, was a pitman. Also signed the pledge. Soon as they brought the beer up in the dumb waiter;

'Howay, we're away!'

Didn't want me dad drinking. Methodist, ye see?'

'He could 'a' been a contender.'

...now, the end is near
And so I face the final curtain
My friend, I'll say it clear
I'll state my case..

'That beer's nae good, if ye wanna kna.'

'What d' ye mean Dad?'

'They've bornt the Broon Ale. Again. Leave the crate there an' I'll take it back. Breweries! Rogues!

I planned each charted course
Each careful step along the byway
And more, much more than this, I did it my way.

Yes, there were times, I'm sure you knew

Good times, Bad Times, I know I've had my share...

When I bit off more than I could chew

But through it all, when there was doubt
I ate it up and spit it out
I faced it all and I stood tall and did it my way

Sid an' Nancy? What a pair. Drugs. That was their trouble. Not like they used a bit of hash. They really ran with it. Heroin. Coke. Anything.

And now, as tears subside I find it all so amusing
To think I did all that
And may I say, not in a shy way
Oh, no, oh, no, not me, I did it my way.

Tears welled up and Col stared ahead before looking down at his son. Siobhan caught his eye and put her hand on her husband's knee. Droplets splashed on the floor below – rain cleansing the dead heat to make way for something different. Repeatedly they splashed, dripping onto a small patch of damp. Aidan poked a pointed index finger and licked the saltiness.

Yes, it was my way.

The curtain closed, purple trimmed with gold tassels. The heat intensified. The furnace roared behind. As Benny Goodman's clarinet supplanted its noise, or Barry Goodman, as the eulogist had called him, Col paused for reflection.
'Come on. They're waiting. Howay Col!'
He was bustled out of the crematorium, Mozart's Clarinet Quintet now resembling the theme music from a film rather than the contemplative theme for which it was intended. Col stood at the door and hugged and kissed

strangers, some of which looked awkwardly on at his familiarity. The sun bleached down on the dampened tarmac outside. Trees, quenched green, dripped droplets onto the road ahead.

'Whoa Davy! Davy! How are you Mate? Sorry to hear aboot yer Grandda'.'

Col winced as Davy looked over at the beaming taxi driver leaning from his Omega. Dance music pumped from within as the sound of Mozart died.

'Come over t' have a look at the flowers. Here. Ower here. They're lovely.'

'Aye, alright. We'll see you in there. Aye. Just ower the road. The Cricket Club.'

'Are you feeling OK Col? Here, have this.'

Siobhan handed him a pint of Scotch and Col sipped without thinking.

'Poor drink that son. Ex. That's the best roond here. Unless ye' can get the real ale. But there's nen o' that roond here. Naebody'll drink it in here either. Keg or tank. A'right by me, mind. Easy to keep. But I prefer the real stuff, mesel'. Like I used to drink. Double Diamond. That was the start of it. When the rot set in.

A terrific draught in here.

Worthy E. Tried gettin' Draught Bass, but its all Worthy E. Ruined it. Stick wi' the tank.

Col headed to the bar next door and away from the crowd. To clear his head. He lit a cigarette and inhaled. The BIC flame danced in unison to his sucking. He held in the smoke before exhaling.

'Pint o' Ex please.'

'We've no Ex. Sorry. Special? That or Trophy.'

'Special please.'

Again, Col inhaled. His heart fluttered and he stood at the bar. Another draught of smoke and his drink sat on the drip tray beneath his chest.

'Have one yerself.'

The barmaid took the blue five pound note and placed it on top of the till tray as it lay open.

'Half o' lager. Thanks.'

'Have a pint if you want.'

'Oh, alright. Thanks.'

The change was placed beside his drink and Col lifted both before heading back to the funeral party next door. Davy walked over to him as he approached Siobhan, addressing them both quietly:

'Arthur's said he wants us to meet up with Frank Armstrong. Said we can meet up anywhere we like. They want to discuss something.'

Chapter 28

Desperate Dan. Dandy. Cow pie. Blow its nose and wipe its arse. That's how I like it.

'Whatever you do Dave, don't let him get to you. Dan. He's a tricky bastard. Can't trust him. He's got the place wrapped up. Or so he thinks.'

'Yeah Siobhan. I know. You're right. Its just that he was always aroond when we were little. Spent a lot of time playing with me, Colin, Richie an' Tommy. Great pool player, and really good at darts.'

'I'm sure. But that's not the point. We can't let this get in the way.'

The road snaked ahead, twisting and turning through the gale driven rain. Rocking back and forth in his seat, Dave stared ahead through the rapid swishing wipers. Jolting and jerking in rhythm with Siobhan's breaking and acceleration. Rain rapidly fell through the beams ahead. Silence, bar the rev and roar of the engine.

Gregg's of Gosforth. Savoury mince and ta-ties. Plate or oval. Cornish.

'I hate those flat pasties. Have ye got any of the real Cornish? No, not the puff pastry ones. The ones with the crimped middle. Shortcrust.'

No Pet. Nen o' them in. Naebody really likes them here. You can have these or what about a meat square? Nice!'

'Aye. Alright, give us one o' the pasties and I'll have a meat square an' all.'

'This one's a bit overcooked. You can have it for nowt, Son.'

Jackman's. That was it. Knew it was something like that. Davy Jackman's. Mate of me uncle's. George, he designed and printed he's menus. Chef's head quartered into different menus. Peas pudding in polystyrene and poured hot like lentil soup. Steaming and swilling. Moustache under a big sneck and big chef's hat.

'Best printer on the Tyne, your George. Great bloke.'

'Wor Geordie's comin' noo.'

'Great.'

'Ye kna, I asked him this mornin' in the Middle Club and he said 'No.''

''Fancy coming to Spain?' I said. Aboot 12 o'clock. Met him again in the Blue Bell doon Jesmond Vale and he said he's comin'. He put a hundred quid on the horses and got a double up. Bought the drinks al' neet. Nearly nine hundred quid he won. Great. Ask him how much he's lost though and he'll not tell ye.'

'Alwi's winnin',' he says.'

'We'll have to get him a room next to we, mind.'

'Divn't worry, he's ganna take care o' that he's sel'.'

'By he's a lucky fucker, wor Geordie.'

'Don't worry Dave. I'll do the talking.'

'No, I'm not worried like that Siobhan. But, its just that he's been such a good friend, you kna? Kna'n him most of me life.'

'Like I said. I'll be nice. I'll be firm though. He'll be fine.'

Fine?

The rain swept them onward towards the bend ahead.

Meandering.

Fine 'n' dandy.

Corky the Cat. Felix. Gnasher.

The Bash Street Kids. Plug ugly. Pugnacious. Teach. Cane. Belt.

'How can you have any pudding if you don't eat yer meat?'

Denis the Menace. Nae softie, him. Fu Fu and Gnasher.

Beezer. Bully, Beef and Chips.

'Are you hungry, Siobhan?'

'Not really. You?'

'No appetite. Not the neet anyway.'

'We can get something in Hexham. If you like. Is there anything there?'

'Not sure. Not really been there much. Never at neet. Prob'ly a chippie there. Or something.'

Something in the way, she moves.
Attracts me like no other lover.

Layla.....

You'll have to have them all pulled out
After the Savoy Truffle.

'Let's put the radio on, should we?'

'Yeah. OK.'

'Radio One? Alright?'

'Aye. Great.'

Ev'rybody wants to rule the world.
d,d,d,d d,d,d d,d, dd...

Darkness. Black. Pitch black.

'Did you see that? There! There, look. Oh, its gone noo.'
'What was it? '
'A roe deer. Bonnie ain an' all. Little antlers.'
'Need to be careful. These roads are deadly. Snaking and twistin'.'

'Alreet Celia?'
'Go ooon Son. Get in there!'
'Shake ya hips.'
'I'm tellin' ye!'
'Ow. Me hair! Get off!'
'Shut it. Now fuck off.'
'Here Davy. Come here. This way. That's it.'
'Put ya hand here. On me hips.'
'Don't be shy.'
'No, don't.'
'Hi ya Ce. Davy.'
'Come here Davy.'
'Oh. Oh, not here Ce. Wait. Ower there. The hothoose.'
'Oh aye. Proper little hothouse floower. A'll be gentle wi' ye.'
'Argh. No Ce. Its me leg. Me ankle.'
'Let's see. Oh. Are you sore there? Oh, its sprained. Its a sprain. I'll get Miss Fulton. Wait here!'
'Aghh! Hurry up Ce.'

These games you play
They're going to end in more than tears some day
Ah-ha Enola Gay
It shouldn't ever have to end this way

Enloa Gay.

'It's the Super Fortress that dropped the atom bomb.'

OMD. Orchestral Manoeuvres in the Dark. More fuckin' Sousers.

Oxygeen.

Mel Gibson. *Gallipoli.* Lions led by donkeys. The Somme. Ypres. *Monocled Mutineer.* Alan Bleasedale. 'Nother Scouser.

Snowy Malone.

'Look at this. The craftsmanship. Nothing like that these days. People just niver take pride in tha' werk.'

'Giza job. Go on Gizit. Go on. I'm Yosser Hughes. A c'n dae that. A'm a brickie! Go on. Gizit.

'What you thinking about Davy? You worried about him?'

'No Siobhan. Honestly. Just thinking aboot the telly. Been watching *Boys from the Blackstuff.*'

'What's that?'

It's a series that's repeated on BBC. Aboot a load o' blokes in Liverpool on the dole.'

'Plenty of that around here.'

'Well aye. But this is from twenty year ago. There was a play done by Alan Bleasedale. He's a Scouser. *The Back Stuff.* I watched it when it first came out with me dad an' Tommy. Great.'

'Anyway, they gan off daein' a guvvie job and get ripped off by a couple a gypsies. Diana Dawes's husband played one o' the Gyppos. This is the sequel. Or sequels. Load o' programmes aboot the lads from the play. An' a couple of others.'

'Good, is it? Must be. You seem to like it.'

'Aye, it is. It's great. Really captured the mood. Like a kitchen sink drama.'

'A what?'

'Kitchen sink drama. That's a distressin' kind o' play. Like a film. Like *Kes*.'

'Oh, that's a good film. Love that. Sad.'

'Aye, well that's a film, but the same type o' thing. These are made for the telly, not the cinema. All aboot life for the doon trodden working class.'

'Down-trodden? Surely you make your own luck, don't you think?'

'What? You're kiddin' aren't ye Siobhan? Nae good luck aroond here. Even made an owld song about it.'

> There's nae good luck in Durham Jail,
> Nae good luck at all.

'Well, that's aboot a jail, but you get the idea.'

'It's a bit like *Auf Wiedersehen, Pet*, is it?'

'A bit. Same sort o' story. But I'd have to say *Auf Wiedersehen's* more like a soap, or a comedy. The' both focus on the workmen and builders, but *The Boys from the Blackstuff* is serious. A drama, I'd say.'

'I watched *Auf Wiedersehen, Pet* back home. Not when it first came out. Just a few years back on video. Colin wanted me to watch it with him. He loved it. Reminded him of home. Nothing like home, I told him. That big ugly one. Not many Geordies like him that I've seen.'

'You mean Oz. There are plenty like him. Especially if you kna where to look.'

'Really? If I'd seen that before I met Colin, I'd probably have ran a mile. Some of them were nice, mind. Neville. And he's mate. The main one. Dennis?'

'Dennis. It was aboot Dennis, Neville and Oz, with a big cast roond them. One of them died after the first series.'

'Really? I thought they all went on to do other stuff.'

'No, the one that played the Cockney. London. Wayne. He used to be a rock star. Been on *Top o' The Pops*. Well he overdosed on heroin. Had to use a double in the second series as he died half way through filming. Real shame.'

'Jimmy Nail, the one that played Oz. Good singer, mind.'

'Yeah, I saw that. In the second series. Country and Western. Love that back home.'

'I always found those programmes about home to be rubbish. *The Quiet Man, The Field*. Full of caricatures. Stereotypes. Usually Yanks' ideas of Ireland. I liked *The Commitments* though.'

'What's that?'

'A film about a group of lads from Tallaght, a big rough council estate near Dublin. A bit cliched, but not bad. Great music.'

'Bit like *The Blues Brothers*?'

'Well, a bit. But no. One of the songs was in *The Blues Brothers*, but no. This was a bit more gritty.'

'More gritty than *Rawhide*? Bottles and cans flyin' everywhere. God, Ireland must be rough.'

'No. I don't mean that. It is just more realistic, if a bit over the top. There's a bit where he's goin' into the lift of the council block and a lad has a knacker horse with him. Funny. And probably true.'

'Really? A horse in a lift?'

'Well, maybe. But the general feel of the film. It seems true to the story. Written by Roddy Doyle. He used to be a school teacher. Must be true, eh?'

'Oh Aye. He'll ha' seen a lot o' hardship then. Not first

hand though.'
'Oh, I don't know. I think he seems alright.'

Chapter 29

'Siobhan, its great to see you. How was the drive?'
Richard eyed his brother and sister-in-law.
'It was OK. Bit bumpy, these roads. Could be back in
Ireland.'
'Oh, surely not that bad.'
Siobhan looked up and down at her host. No pleasure to
be mixed with business tonight. Coolly, candidly, she
spoke deliberately.
'Where is he? When's he coming?'
'What? Come on, I thought you might..'
'Never mind what you thought.'
'Come on, I've got a little spread set up. We're having
Chinese. You like that don't you? I mean, surely even the
Irish like Chinese food. Or is that too cosmopolitan?'
Siobhan fought back an urge to swear at her brother-in-
law. Again she regarded him coolly and uttered as few
words as she needed to instil in him the gravity of the
day.
'Look, I'm sure you mean well Rich, but I have been on
my feet all day, and I had to drive here tonight. I just
need to rest, and maybe get something light. No big fuss.'
'What, its no trouble. I know Dan'll be wanting to meet
up with you ower there. He's been looking forward to
meeting with you. Dave, How are you man?
'Fine.' Dave looked away and then at the ground.
Ten thirty-five. The school-clock over the bar ticked, the
only sound in the room, vivid white face, Roman

numerals surrounded by an oak cabinet suspended amid the entirely oak panelled room. Siobhan stared up at Richard as he looked uncomfortably from her face to his brother and back again. Empty and almost silent, the bar's internal door opened and in walked a tall slender man, hair slicked into a fifties DA, quaffed, he gave the appearance of an ageing cultivated Teddy Boy.

'Siobhan. How are you? How's it going? Are you going to have a drink?'

'Just water. We'll both have water. That's OK, Dave?'

'Oh, aye Siobhan. Fine.'

'But we were going to head over to the Chinese over the road. Maybe you'd like that.'

'No, I was just saying to Rich. We are only here to get down to business in the morning before heading back. We've got a lot to get through, so I need an early night. Been up all day. Tired.'

'No, that's fine with us.'

'Sure you don't fancy it Dave? I could introduce you to a couple of girls I know. Like that wouldn't you? Always had an eye for the ladies. Maybe go out dancing later on. Decent club roond the corner.'

'No, I'm OK Dan. Early night.'

'Just like Siobhan then?'

Dan eyed them both before pouring himself a whisky and Coke. He placed it on the counter and then added two half pint glasses of water.

'Here you go.'

Dave handed Siobhan her glass and took a sip of his water before sitting next to her.

'We thought you might come up with a fair price for the hotel Dan. Have a think about what it might be worth, and we'll have a chat about it. I'll get our solicitor to put something down on paper and we can finalise something next week.'

The clock ticked for more than a few seconds as Dan stared down at her.

'What do you mean, a fair price? I'm not selling. Quite happy here.'

'We thought you might like to move on. I mean things aren't exactly rosy, are they? It seems like your business is under performing year on year. So have a think about it.'

'Listen, I'm not leaving and that's it. Who the fuck do you think you are? Coming here and tryin' to push me around. I've been nothing but nice to Jerry and he's family. For years I put up with his whinin' and complainin'.'

'Why did you humiliate Rich last month then? Don't you go around pushing us around like that. Never again, I tell you.'

'What? Siobhan, come on,' interposed Rich. 'That was nothing. Nothing at all. Just a little misunderstanding. We are best of pals. Aren't we Dan?'

'Yeah. Course. But you have to see it from my point of view. He'd been slackin' lately. Not really puttin' he's back in to it. I just straightened him out. All done and dusted.'

'Yeah. That's right. No problem.'

Rich hugged his friend.

'Have a nice rest ladies.' Dan swilled the drink down and turned to leave. 'You coimin' Richard?'

'I'll be out in a minute Dan. See you over there.'

Dave, stared down at the floor in front, Siobhan sipped from the water.

'Fuck's sake Siobhan! What you daeing? You divn't

come ower to Hexham and say something like that to Dan Robson. Of all people. He's been very good to we all.'

'Listen Richard. I don't care what's happened today. But remember that I am in charge now. Don't go around taking other people's side in front of other people.'

'What you on aboot. You're the new ain here. Who the fuck do you think ye are? Dave?'

Dave looked at the floor.

'What the fuck ye on Man? Why you gannin' on like this? Where's Col? Shouldn't ye be back at hyem wi' ya bairn?'

'Never mind about Colin or Aidan. They're both back home. We are here on business. Now let's get to bed. You better get over to see Dan. And be careful.'

Chapter 30

Sun sweltered the city, and Siobhan walked through High Bridge, heels clacking on the cobbled road as she headed in the direction of Gray Street. Boutiques and bars, either side of her, contrasted sharply with the surroundings she had become used to viewing as premises in and around her family's Northumberland business. Along with the family's competition, and this was how she viewed all the local businesses around Alnwick, not enough was available to allow any business to thrive. For all the pathos that Northumberland deserved, and there was lots, Siobhan, as an outsider, could clearly see that a clean break, a fresh start, was necessary. Well not necessarily totally fresh, but as near as could effectively be. Her drive into the centre of Newcastle, the region's capital, away from the ancient Northumbrian capital of Bamburgh, was where the new focus should be. Today, would be the start of this new beginning.

Turning left, the sun glinted as Siobhan pulled her sunglasses from her head and down onto her eyes. The sandstone buildings, curving downward towards the railway bridge on Dene Street, snaking further onto the Quayside, rosy in their aspect, offered newfound promise. She waited on the flagged pavement, the cashpoint in use by another young woman. She surveyed the street again, below and above. The Monument, Earl Grey shining in the sun above, seemed pivotal to the community, and although there were occasions when people could ascend to its balcony on top, Siobhan felt that she was in need of no fresh perspective. All had come to her in the weeks prior, and she purused the new vision without doubt. This monument, contrasting sharply with the proposed memorial to her late father-in-law in his home town, assured her the grandeur of Newcastle would afford her and the business far more opportunities. A big fish in a big pond. The City could provide her and the family with the direction it had been needing for so long.

1113. The cash machine accepted her verification and she ordered enough money to see her comfortably conclude the weekend's business.

'Hello. Celia. Where are you?'

'Yeah. OK. I'll meet you there then. See you in twenty minutes.'

Siobhan pulled the phone from her ear, stared down at its green screen and snapped it shut.

'That girl can teach me a few things.'

Siobhan turned and continued walking down the street. Optimism, something she'd been struggling with until the last few months, was now flooding her mind as the street shone in the sunlight. The glare, filtered somewhat by the dark lenses, remained vivid, if somewhat tamed and manageable. She sauntered and noticed young men turning to look at her as she proceeded downhill.

Smiling, she proceeded further until she reached the lights on Collingwood Street. She looked around and amid the traffic rushing either way she took in the buzz of the Toon. St Nicholas' Cathedral, just visible across the road to her right, the BT tower contrasting in style on her left. The last time she had been here was during the fight in Don Vito's. She'd hurried out of there quick. She never really had a chance to take a look around. But she could see that this was a nice area. Fights happen everywhere.

She crossed the road as the pelican blared. Oblivious to those around her, she reached the kerb and angled forty five degrees towards the far side of Dene Street. Yes. This was the place. Glass fronted, the white framed windows spanned upwards onto two floors. A circular turret, coniclal slate roof, clearly dilapidated and white framed windows boarded up sat above the front upper window stretching in front of the acutely angled roof behind it. Although this fearture was present above two other of the Victorian terraces that Siobhan was looking at, both up hill and down, the one above the facade she was about to enter was the only one in such a dilapidated state.

She walked down and reached into the white framed glass door, offset into the two curved bays. She looked down into her purse and pulled the keyring out from its inside pocket. The Yale turned and she stepped inside.

In front of her, the place gleamed as black and silver metal stared from on top of the bar. A Newly installed coffee machine - Gaggia. Italy's best, and a fitting focal point. To the right of the bar, a passage through to the back. The well presented bar area opened to a less presentable room behind. Enough room to seat thirty easily. A spiral staircase, about a dozen steps to the room above led to the mezzanine. Again, enough room to cope with any busy Saturday night. A further dozen steps reached up to the ceiling.

She turned back and walked over to the spiral stairs and looked down into the cellar. She unhooked the chain, accessing the black wrought iron steps, and carefully descended the spiral into the space below. She counted. Eleven steps between each of the three floors in a continual spiralling flight ascending up to the ceiling. At first she had worried that the staircase may not pass regulations, but had been assured that this had been installed well before the regulations had applied, and had served the restaurant for many years. She had organised a further staircase at the back of the ground floor. This would ensure compliance, and indeed the place had passed the inspection. Connections. Not quite the complete break from Jerry's legacy.

Beneath, in the darkness, the air, dank and pungent, sprung to life as three spot-lights switched on. With every movement dust flared and danced within their beams. Piles of smashed and opened bottles sat in crates or lay strewn amongst the empty kegs, some of which had been opened in the centre. The lift, half laden with crates, sat waiting to be hoisted above and into the bar. Someone had clearly abandoned the building in a hurry. As she picked her way through the gloom and opened the cooler door, she recoiled on touching the wet corpse of something. She shrieked as she realised a rat had recently decomposed on the shelf.

Looking into the cooler she was horrified at the devestation within. Among the half dozen kegs lay the pipes. Broken bulbs had leaked stale beer all over the place and two gas cylinders lay sideways, one propped up partly by a keg, the other flat on the floor. The stench of dried beer made Siobhan's eyes water and she gagged, turning back to the door. Whincing, she exited and moved back to the foot of the staircase, ascending to the floor above.

She stepped over to the bar and moved through the doorway and into the room behind. Grease and grime, filthy mouldering cooking implements and crockery were strewn everywhere, much of it broken and shattered on the damp moderately sized kitchen floor within. Rat shit peeped from under the work surfaces. Why he'd put up such a fight as she wrested control of this place, she could not now understand. But she was about to turn the place around, no matter how much ground work was needed.

'Hallow. Hallo. Siobhan.' Celia was here.

'Celia. Through here.'

Celia could be heard upstairs as she moved towards the staircase. Siobhan headed over towards it so they could meet up in front of the bar.

'Fuckin' Hell. What a dump this is Siobhan. Are ye sure aboot this? Not much of a beginning, is it?'

Siobhan looked up the staircase as her younger friend descended.

'I think it will be great when it is cleaned up and we have spent a bit of time on the renovations.'

'Aye, well I think you might be reet. The staircase is lovely anyway. How ye ganna to set the place oot? Nae good like this. The place never really took off bifore. Jerry never really got much rent from anyone.'

'This time, Celia, we'll make the place work ourselves.'

'This place is fuckin' filthy Siobhan. But I think it'll scrub up al'reet.'

'Not sure about the spiral staircase. Can't see what use that is.'

'Well its ornamental, isn't it?'

'Takes up a load of space.'

The front of the bar was indeed seemingly encumbered by the dilapidated stairway. Once white and pristine, now this was no longer in use for the upper areas and supplanted by the health and safety compliant back stairs, all flights of which gave unimpeded access to the upper and lower floors, as well as, more importantly, a means of exit in the case of an emergency.

'I think it will be best if we get rid of it, Its a white elephant. I could get more customers in here if this thing was moved out. It serves no purpose. It's redundant.'

'Listen Siobhan. I know you can't see the situation as it is at the minute, but look at how lovely the spiral is. Look.'

'Where Celia? I don't see what you mean.'

'I know the iron work is a rusted and the paintwork needs strippin' off and repainting. But believe me, this is ganna look great.'

Celia stepped onto the bottom two steps as if to reascend to the next upper floor. The frame shook. She persisted. Flakes of paint fluttered to the ground and settled amongst the dust below as she ascended slowly. With each step the frame rattled and clanked.

'Careful Celia. You're gonna bring the whole thing down. Its collapsing!'

'No Siobhan. These things are built to last. Probably ower a hundred year owld.'

'Listen Ce. Don't worry about it. Its not that important. I need to think of the bigger picture here. And the old spiral staircase isn't where it's at. Come down. We'll forget about it for now.'

Siobhan walked behind the bar again. Stained and strewn with rubbish, the narrow floor, its broken tiles contrasting with her white stilettos, showed signs that, like the rest of the bar area, much needed to be done to return the place to its original Victorian grandeur. Although the massive front windows, rising and framing both the ground and first mezzanine floors, were clearly later in period to the original building, Siobhan recognised the potential. The Gaggia, clearly a much later addition, and in seeming disrepair, could be brought to life again. A great feature and not out of place in any restaurant bar around this upper Quayside area.

Celia looked over the rail, as if overlooking a balcony, and looked down at her older friend.

'Look at this up here Siobhan. Dirty bastards! These have been here years. Johnnies. Loads of them. Loads o' needles an' all.'

'Celia. For God's sake! Get down. Be careful. Watch what you're stepping on. Filth.'

'I'll come back doon the spiral.'

'I think the place is great after all Siobhan. Absolutely brilliant! Loads o' room to expand oot.'

'Let me organise everything wi' the staircase, will ye? I can alri'dy see it Pet.'

Siobhan looked over the disconnected cobwebbed beer taps towering over the floor below, three dirty broken tiles in the middle of the floor, and wondered when the place could be ready. How would she manage this move? It certainly looked ambitious at the minute, but it was obvious that there was potential here. And the whole area was ripe for opening out. Footfall, all important to any venture, showed this was the place. She just had to convince everyone else.

That staircase though. That's another story.

Chapter 31

Now that the premises had been cleaned up and all the rubbish removed the place seemed cavernous by comparison to a fortnight ago. Local tradesmen and jobbing builders and labourers all jumped at the opportunity of working, especially without the need for bringing in their P45s. Siobhan attended the premises on a daily basis and surveyed progress. She was seen as a fair minded boss, focused and polite, but absent most of the time. Celia, on the other hand, attended the premises throughout, and was sometimes accompanied by Gillian, who was focused less on working in the Queen's Head, and was getting to know what would become her new workplace. Most of the time it was Gillian who attended to the decorating of the bar area whist the lads worked out back on the painting and carpentry.

The staircase, clearly not part of the original structure, was an enigmatic feature and not altogether practical, except as the only entry into the cellar area. Along with the double doored hatch in front of the left sided window, it was the only way into the cellar. Fortunately, once the old barrels and crates had been removed and sent back to the brewery, and the pipework and cooler had been repaired, the space was spartan but workable. Hardly massive, but sufficient to house around a dozen barrels, ample crates of soft drinks and plenty of bottled beer and wine boxes.

The luckiest part was that the cooler had taken virtually

no work in fixing. Although not currently in operation, there was nothing to keep cool, Gillian had kept it running for a morning and proven that the cool room was working effectively and reliably.

The lift. That had proven more difficult. The old lift frame and floor had rotted and the old rope had perished so it was easier to have a new one installed than try to repair the existing lift. A new one had been installed with a shaft that could be accessed from the kitchen behind the bar. This would allow staff to operate a dumb waiter up to the mezzanine and the lift doors made into a modest feature where the food could also be served on the upper floor. Siobhan had been instrumental in the idea, although it had been left to Gillian to finalise the details. It was an impressive set-up.

Like everything, Siobhan was proving great on ideas and could lead by inspiration. Details were not her strong point though, and the two women around her took care of the details, delegating to the workers around them. Promoted from within the family business; Gillian, older and proven as diligent, reliable and able; Celia, a less obvious choice, but great to have around as a confident third eye. Only Davy remained of the original management team now, and he could always be relied on to help in any capacity required. Steady and stable, as always, he had begun to think he was being frozen out of his birthright. Siobhan had been mindful of his insecurity and made repeated ostentatious attempts at reassurance. Time was now proving that things were working out for him and all around him.

Celia was in no doubt as to the potential of what she saw as the premises' greatest single asset. Although not particularly practical in regards present day regulations, this historical feature, still used to descend to the cellar, was to be a focal point of the restaurant layout. Even though most would be barred from using its upper flights, the spiral was to be the entrance to the new office. And she was determined to surprise Siobhan, who was as yet unaware of her young friend's plans.

Not having trusted the stability of the staircase, Siobhan had not ventured above the mezzanine, and was unaware what was awaiting her discovery up there barring the dilapdated space within the attic. Celia was going to ensure the unexplored area would be a perfect management office, a fitting start to the new business. Siobhan, with her new ideas and willingness to act on them, would secure the family business for another generation, and Celia was excited about what the future held. Done right, this restaurant, with its ideal city centre location on the way to and from the Quayside, would be a perfect bridging point between the river and the Bigg market, Newcastle's world famous party area. Siobhan was right to try to attract clientele here, and Celia similarly saw success ahead.

She had first ventured up the rickety steps when first alone in the restaurant. Siobhan saw little of interest and assumed, as did everyone else, that they led nowhere interesting. Celia's natural intuition, or was it curiosity, had led her to the top. As she ascended the steps, all thirty three of them, she discovered a trap door had been covered by some renovation work in the past. Some previous owner saw the attic, or whatever it was, as surplus to requirements, as did Siobhan. Celia felt differently and pushed the ceiling gypsum. Nothing happened, except the rocking and shaking of the stair frame below. Quite frightening, but not enough to perturb her. After some persistence Celia broke through and ascended to open the shuttered windows above.

Chapter 32

'Thanks a lot Celia. What is it?'
'You'll have to wait and see, won't you? And don't open it until you get back.'
'What? Come on! Let me open it now. What's the point of waiting till I'm back. You'll get no benefit from my seeing it. That's the best part of giving a present.'

Better to give than to receive. Back in front of the altar. Mother took her religiously – maybe not – but at least a couple of times a month. Lots of pressure to attend, and her mother was a bit of a conformist. Couldn't be anything else back home in Leitrim, lovely Leitrim, although she managed to resist the weekly attendance.
'I'll put a bit extra in next time.'
'When's Dad back?'

'That's great Celia. I love it. Very nice.'
The elder woman laughed and pulled the item from the box. Long and segmented, it was lifted carefully from the polystyrene packaging.
'Oh, there are three bits.'
She looked down and pulled the other two pieces, placed them on the table before her and pulled apart the bottom layer of the packaging box. Inside was a small triangular plastic plate-like piece.
'This is just like a spade, I mean ace of spades type.'
'Look at the other pieces in there Siobhan.'

She pulled out the other piece, a small shapely plastic piece.

'What's this? Is it another pelvis?'

'Not exactly. Take a good look. Can you see what it is?'

'These pieces, I initially thought you had got me a snake skeleton, but I realise now that they are three pieces of a backbone. This is a pedestal, obviously. This piece must be the base of the spine. Coccyx, isn't it? And this little pelvis. That's what this is, is it?'

'Well not quite Pet.'

Siobhan took the little pelvis and held it. Turning it around in her hands, looking closely and scrutinsing the bone.

'Look, hold it like this.'

Holding up the model of the backbone Celia grabbed the piece and held it in front of her friend before slowly hovering the bone above it.

'Look, it fits on top of this top section like this.' She turned the two pieces to face Siobhan and showed her the top of the model spine.

There are eleven vertebrates in each section. And this piece on top. What does it look like?

'A drgon fly?'

'Look more carefully Pet.'

Siobhan took the model and pieced together the three sections of vertebrate, each fitting easily together as per manufacture.'

'Its lovely Ce. Thanks a lot. I'll have a closer look at home.'

'No. Noo ye've got it oot, put it together prop'ly. Here.'

Celia handed the base section and handed it to Siobhan, who affixed it to the bottom section of the model spine, below the coccyx and pelvis.

'I still cant figure out the dragonfly thing. How does it go on?'

Celia took the model from her friend and fixed the pieces together.

'Oh. It is the top of a snake after all.'

'No. It's not. Its the human spine al'reet. See this top piece. This is the part that is in the base of yer skull. The piece holds your brain in place. And yeah. It does look like a dragonfly.'

'If you look at it more closely, you can see it looks like a butterfly and look at it from the front. It actually looks like the face of an owl.'

'Oh, yeah. It does. I never realised this was in the head. I thought the skull was just a single bone.'

'Well no, this is the central part of the head, at the top of the spine.

This piece holds your brain in place. It is the key to everything. Look, some people say it looks like the fangs of the snake, but it is the monarch. The monarch butterfly. The key to all consciousness, they say.'

Celia picked up the model and finally reattached it on the pole she'd placed into the top central point of the cuboid base.

'Oh, God, thanks. You've had it engraved.'

As above, so below. That is the key to everything in the universe Siobhan. As above, so below.'

Peering carefully at the small plaque, a tiny ingot, she read:

AS ABOVE SO BELOW

Celia and Siobhan,
Together

on the
Stairway to Heaven

'Well it's lovely Ce. Definitely different.'
'Look, I just thought it would be nice for yer new office. I've got to be away, but there's a lot more to it than this. Its not just a model, and I'll leave ye with it. Think of it as a puzzle. I'll meet up with ye later in the week and I'll explain aboot it a bit more. Its ganna literally blow your mind.'
Celia stood up, collected her purse and phone from the table in front of them and bent over, kissing her elder friend lightly on the cheek with a friendly peck.

Chapter 33

Man in the moon. What rubbish.

Siobhan stared at the moon above. Vivid, bright and haloed. It shone intensely and seemed much bigger than normal. Harvest moon. Hunter's moon. Whatever it was, it seemed to herald something in her that she was vaguely aware of, but which she was unable to place a finger on.

She thought of her dead mother in her grave back in Carrick. Adjacent to the famine graves, but well-kept and tidied. At least until her departure.

'Turns people mad. Full moon. Lunacy, they say.'

'Rubbish Ma. How can it?'

'The tides are controlled by the moon, so why do you think it doesn't control or have some kind of hold on us Siobhan? Stands to reason. The power of the Moon.'

The Cortina roared up the road, top o' the range.

'Better t' get them in England. Higher spec.'

'Can we afford to be wasting money on a new car? There's not enough money to keep us over here.'

'Listen Luv. I had a bit put by, and I got a good deal. Part exchanged the other one. We'll not notice the difference.'

'Put by. What do you mean? Put by? We've had barely enough to eat here, and you're swanning off to England. Galivantin' in London. What do you think goes on over here when you're over there?'

'Oh, shut up Beck will ye? Keep on goin' on. All the time its somethin'.'

'You keep sayin' you'll send money back. Where is it? Waiting for you, that's all I seem to be at. Waiting. Such a disappointment. And now ye turn up in a brand new car. We're starvin' here.'

The moon shone and Siobhan looked down at the sea. The stirring breakers gradually receded into still wavy lines, illumined monochrome, daylight without shadow.

That girl was a funny one. Funny ideas. How could she believe in all that stuff? Mumbo jumbo.

'Ce, if there's any truth in it you should be able to tell me my star sign, shouldn't you?'

'So, what is it?'

Never come across a charlatan able to predict accurately. Always some vague notion. Predictions. My arse!

A lucky guess. And anyway, Celia already knew about her birthday. When it was. She probably asked Col. Or even Aidan.

Celia had been going on about her interest in all things spiritual for a while now. Said that was why she was such a 'free spirit.' Never shut up about it now though. Always going on about it. Astrology. Never could get me head round it. At least a lot of people were into that. Even the papers printed it everyday. So it is harmless, I expect. But tarot readings, crystals. Numerology? What is that all about?'

'You've got numbers throughout your life and they are assigned to you naturally by your birth time and date. And where you were born, naturally. A bit like astrology, it works with your birth phases.'

'Can't understand it Ce. Seems like a lot of work, working it all out.'

'What do you think of the jobs the lads are doing then?'

'They're great. Great work. 'Specially Alan. Very good with he's hands, I expect.'

'Celia, I'm not joking. What do you think? Can you give it a rest for a minute and think about the restaurant? Please?'

'Come on Pet. Divn't be so stuck up. I've got iv'rything in hand. Really. Gillian's there an' all. She thinks things are shapin' up well an' all. Don't worry.'

Worry. Never done anything but worry.

'Dad's not back yet?' Its my birthday tomorrow, and he's not back. Is he coming?'

'Well I think he's been tied up at work Love. He'll probably be sending you a card over with some money. He needs the work and can't keep nipping over all the time. You understand don't you?'

'Understand? Mam. I wasn't even expectin' him over. But he was the one making all the promises. 'Promise, promise, promise. He's a dick, Ma'. A proper dick.'

'Siobhan. That's your father you're referring to. Now stop that. Your father loves you very much. But he's got lots on, I expect.'

'Alright Pet?'

Siobhan turned and saw a middle aged couple passing, their faces discernible clearly in the moonlight.

'Hi there. Lovely night.'

She turned and again looked out beneath the Moon. A ship was moving into view. Making its way into the mouth of the river, it grew. Larger and larger. Smoke billowed from the two funnels. She watched as it was met by the smaller pilot, which turned and led the tanker through the beacons on the harbour walls either side and into the river. Vast and rapid, the boat disturbed the flotilla of moored boats in its wake. They bounced and rocked as the wave passed them, gradually returning to a calm stand-still. The stern of the tanker raced on up the river.

'You wanna watch her ye kna' Siobhan. She's a bit of a funny ain.'

Celia had been anything but problematic. If it hadn't been for her young friend, her love of life, and her friendliness, which allowed her to mingle with and be comfortable with anyone, Siobhan knew this venture would never have taken off. Was she right to trust to this instinct? Was there a chance she was barking up the wrong tree? That she was making a mistake.

Gillian, ever reliable and dependable, the backbone of Jerry's bar, she would keep Celia's youthful enthusiasm in check; if that's what it could be called. She would look after everything.

'Yeah. I love Celia. But she can be a bit of a handful. When she's not reigned in properly.'

'Perhaps Gillian. That's why I want you to keep an eye on her. And things in the bar. Will you do that?'

'What do you mean?'

'Well just that. I want you to keep an eye on the progress at the bar. Just keep an eye on things. Make sure all is running well. And just look after things with Celia.'

'You want me to spy on her Siobhan? Spy on Celia?'

'I never said that Gill. But look. I need an assistant manager, and you would be best placed to fill the role. Don't you think?'

'Oh, Siobhan. Are you promoting me here?'

'Gillian. Come on. Hardly a promotion is it? You've been

pretty much looking after everything at the Queen's Head. This time, though, you'll get the pay and recognition to go with it.'

'Its a bit of a trek. I don't know.'

'I'm sure we can work something out there. We can factor that into your overall salary package. You can take a company car or have the money. We could even get you a bus and Metro pass if you'd prefer.'

'What aboot Davy? He's a good lad you know.'

'Don't worry about Davy. I know he's great. I'll make sure he's taken care of. He'll be happy enough, I'm sure.'

'And Celia? What'll she think of me bossin' her around? Me not part o' the family, like?'

'Again, let me worry about her. Just you keep an eye on her, and be subtle. She's a great girl. I'm really taken with her.'

'Aye. That's Celia. Naturally good with people. Knows exactly how to keep everybody happy. She had Tommy wrapped roond her little finger, ye kna'.'

'Yes. Davy and Col both said they had a bit of a thing going on.'

'If that's what you wanna call it.'

Around the corner, followed by intermittent strong and weak light, two men hurried along the kerbside. Pulling bins from the footpath and onto the roadside, they worked in tandem passing Siobhan as she sat on the bench.

'Al' reet there?'

'Hello. Lovely night.'

The man's amber face faded as he turned and raced up the road. His companion scurried alongside the large bin lorry, accompanied by another man, placing onto and removing the bins from the back of the wagon. The noise, clattering and grinding, faded slowly along with the hued figures alongside the truck. It turned the bend and gradually disappeared.

'Geordie. Hurry up! Ower there.'

The moon resumed its monochrome hue and Siobhan looked out to the North Sea again, watching the approach of the incoming ferry. Nightly, it arrived before heading back to Norway, then on to Sweden. An ancient route linking the North East with the outside. Another route which failed to diminish or dilute the region's unique identity. Funnels billowed and the boat's approach was accompanied by an increase in engine roar.

Siobhan stood, threw away her cigarette into the roadside gutter, twisted her shoe's sole side to side on top before turning away from the riverside and heading back over to her car.

'Yer lucky naebody broke into yer car, Pet. I've been watchin' it and already two groups o' lads have been sniffin' aboot it. Ye wanna be careful. It's the stereo. Worth a fortune.'

'Oh. Is it not safe round here then?'

'Aye Pet. Safe, but not for the car. They're breaking into them cars all the time. Them stereos, they're aboot three hundred quid each. The kids roond here just smash the windaes and scarper with them.'

'Well thanks. I never knew that. I'll be careful in future.'

'Ye dae that Pet. Never leave ya car like that roond here.'

'Thanks.'

Siobhan turned away from the man and opened the door. The interior, black leather throughout was obviously a target, now she came to think of it. But for just the cassette player. Sony. Top of the range. Yes. It made sense. All it would take would be a brick and in 2 minutes the stereo would be gone. To think of it. Easy pickings for some young scally. How this one had lasted so long was beyond her.

The engine fired and Siobhan released the ignition key. The portable CD player lit up and track seventeen started. A faint hum came from the player, connected into the main cassette player by a small wire on the end of a fake audio cassette. Tapes were always fine, but everything is CDs these days. Shame to get rid of this stereo, though. Great sound quality.

Voodoo People. Prodigy.

Col never tired of this stuff.

She switched on the radio.

> 'I mean, this is, you kna, I'll make sure we all, you know, gan the whole hog. It's, whatever it is, is there and there's so many people that 'ave actually witnessed things like that so it's, I mean, there may well be truth in it. I want to ask Jewel.'
>
> 'We'll do polls, they are a little bit later on, because this is *Nightowls* on Metro Radio.'

Lucky escape. Never even thought of that. The car, its got an immobiliser. Even thought of getting a tracker, the insurance recommended it, I think. But the stereo. Makes sense. Three hundred quid. Get a lot of drinks on that. Even if they got a hundred and fifty. God. Just break into a couple a night and never need to work again. Plenty of places to sell them on. Plenty of second hand shops and stuff.

Bet Celia could enlighten me there. Bet she could.

'Howay Siobhan. Lets gan. We need to be away if we're gonna get the Metro back.'

'Ce, I really feel great. Can't believe this. Amazing! Feckin' amazing. Feck! Feck! Where d'y get these from?

'Ye divn't wanna kna, Pet.'

'I think you're fecking ace, Celia. Feckin' ace! ACE!!'

'Aye al' reet Pet. I think ye might need to have a swig o' this water. Here. No, not too much. Just a bit.'

'Forget the Metro. Lets stay out. Anywhere else to go. Where d'ye recommend?'

'There's the Global Village. Just opened. Got some good reviews, I can tell ye. Music's good. A tenner in though.'

'Great. Let's go there.'

'Another one here forst?'

'Yeah. I'm not having more water though. Lets have Becks.'

'Two pints o' Becks please.'

The road bent ahead and Siobhan manoeuvred the saloon with it, steering slowly into the road as it snaked past the terraces on the left, garage on her right. Around she travelled before ascending to view the small harbour ahead. Bridging the valley below her, the road swept onwards towards Wallsend and Siobhan wondered at the contrasting poverty around. Was this venture prudent? Could she safely take this risk, banking everything on this place? What did she know about the area? Look at it. Desolate and deprived. Is there enough money to spare to let her eke out a living here? Does she want to go down the same road of her father-in-law. Once a successful local businessman. Pillar of the local community. Finished up with hardly anyone in his place. Just Arthur, his family and the staff. And a few locals. Was it a good idea to set down here?

> 'So she went to that school forty-eight years ago or so. The headmaster then was called Mr Guy, and we were wondering if that was a player you were talking about. You know, it might be he got photographs and money when he was living there. Photographs of when he was delivering..'

Dad's photo. Hung in the front room. Only image she could recall now. Bigger than everyone on the estate. That had impressed Mam. Her big protector. Fat chance! Never away from England. Marriage of inconvenience. On Ma's side. Plenty of convenience for him, though. Never took responsibility. Ever.
Poor Ma!
Janice. That's her name. Could be anywhere. Could be here. There or anywhere. Prick! Half sister. Somewhere in England. Wild Irish Rover.
Least neither of us got any money afterwards.
Prick!

Segedunum. Wallsend. Old building site left. Old battlements opposite. The car sped past and approached the blue flashing lights heading towards Siobhan on the opposite side. Approaching, the lights began to flare and the siren increased in strength. Siobhan tensed as it approached. The Rover ahead blared, two officers alert inside, one looking ahead, the other surveying Siobhan, turning her head as they sped past. Siobhan sighed and proceeded, accelerating away from the noise and blue flashing lights. Silence ensued again. Silence until she picked up again the sound of the radio.

> '....and that is my nifty little link into a commercial great in the tail of Halley's Comet. Houston we have a problem. There's something wrong. We have an artificial obstacle. Something. Nature something. Something hungry.
> I'm the director of prototypes...'

Weirdos. Feckin' eejits! Siobhan pressed the scanner on the radio and silence again ensued. She switched on the wipers. She thought of Celia as they squeaked softly and picked up the rain on the blades until silence again reigned.
Celia. Now there's a risk. Is she a risk worth taking?

Chapter 34

She really was lovely, but strange, no doubt.
Siobhan sat looking at the model kindly donated by her younger friend and relative. She really was puzzled by the gift, but grateful at another piece of thoughtfulness from her.
They had been growing increasingly close since the first meeting in Newcastle, and Siobhan felt she had been introduced to Northumberland and particularly Newcastle in a way impossible had their friendship not blossomed. The younger woman, so much more womanly than herself, had gone about welcoming Siobhan with open arms. Celia, although far less travelled and less cosmopolitan, was nevertheless much more worldly than her older friend. And fun to be around. Siobhan had found herself spending less and less time with Colin and Aidan in order to be around her, and to be part of the scenes in Alnwick and Newcastle.

She picked up the pieces and held them in turn. The first eleven vertebrate she attached so that the bottom and middle sections fitted perfectly. She fitted them onto the pole and threaded it into the top of the base.
'Stairway to Heaven. What does it mean?' she thought.
Led Zeppelin?

'Here Mate. On the corner. One Chatsworth Gardens, aye.'

The two women exited the taxi and headed up the steps to the black door above.

'Fuck! I don't know Celia. I should have been on my way back, really. I wish I could get him on the phone. I hope he'll be all right. What about Aidan?'

'It'll be al'reet Siobhan. He's a good lad, Col. Always liked him. Really nice bloke. You cannit drive all the way back, not in the state you're in. An' a taxi'll cost a fortune. Ring him again, and I'll get us some glasses. Gan into that bureau ower in the corner, will ye? There's a bag o' weed in there.'

'Oh, fuck it, eh? I'll roll one up and then I'll try him again. Have you got any matches?'

'On top o' the fireplace. There. There's a lighter.'

Siobhan lay back on the couch. Another drag and she relaxed to the music. Celia sat hunched on the armchair opposite, and took the joint from Siobhan.

'This tack is great. Get it from a mate roond the corner. He's a bit of a'reet, an' all.'

She pursed her lips around the cigarette and sucked. She addressed Siobhan through clenched teeth, her voice strained as she held the smoke before exhaling deeply. She paused, looked down at the joint and took another drag.

'Here. Here Siobhan. Ye a'reet? Want this?'

'Never better Ce.'

Siobhan rose on one elbow and reached over, taking it with her left hand from Celia.

'Ha' ye never heard o' the third eye Siobhan? Most people divn't kna aboot it Man, so yer alreet. Listen. Ye can look through yer eyes as normal, but there are other ways o' seein'. The third eye. Its inside your heed, behind the top o' your nose. Ye kna them Indian lasses wear the red spot.

Well that is meant to be the third eye. Eastern mystics.'
'This is more of your New Age stuff, is it Ce? I heard you were into that. C'mon then. Let's hear it then.'
'Everyone has it, and we all use it all the time, 'specially when we're young, though you'll probably ha' forgot. Listen. You can be retrained to use it.'
'The Monarch. Remember, the model, and the top o' the spine. That is the key that holds ivr'ything. I tell't ye' aboot it bifore. Remember, I said t' ye: "As above, so below." Remember, the model. Th' inscription?'
'I was reading the inscription on the stand Ce. Wondering about it. What ye on about?'
'Here.' Siobhan winked over at her companion and held forth the joint for Celia.
'The Beatles. Ye kna? *Hard Days Neet, She Loves Ye.* All that poppy shite they did. Mind, *She Loves Ye* was written in the Toon. When they were here on tour.'
'Well if ye' listen to their later stuff, and its great, mind, well they start getting into India. They went off with this Yogi guy. Maharishi. Aye, he torned oot to be a perv, they says. But he was meant to be onto sommick. Used to teach them meditation. Transcendental meditation.'
'Well they were learning how to open up the third eye. George Harrison. He was the best lookin' one. Though I'd dae them all – mebe not Ringo, but niver mind.'
'Anyway, they were all in India and they were findin' oot aboot the third eye. Meditation lets you see the world, the universe, ev'rything, as it really is. Lookin' through the Monarch. The wise old owl.'
'That's what got me into it. I love the Beatles.'

Hey, Jude, don't make it bad
Take a sad song and make it better

Remember to let her into your heart
Then you can start to make it better

'Ye kna that one? Here.'
Siobhan reached and grabbed the spliff.
'Anyway they really are great. I'll lend you this. *Sergeant Pepper*. Proper druggies.'

When you've seen beyond yourself then you may find
Peace of mind is waiting there
And the time will come when you see we're all one

And life flows on within you and without you.

'Imagine if you walked roond iv'rywhere in sunglasses and all of a sudden you took them off. Everything looks different all of a sudden. That's shiftin' Karma. Beatles were bang into it.'
'Couple o' year ago I started getting' migraines. Noo ye gan to the doctor and she gives you tablets. That's what they dae. Well I had been reading up on it, and I thought "Fuck it!" I'll not take them any more. Oh, I started being light sensitive, and had a ting-lin' in me forehead. Just behind, above me eyes. Felt a bit like a tickin' clock. Ticking all the time for weeks. Couldn't sleep or nowt. After a bit langer I started getting swirling colours. Purples, reds, greens. Light at forst, but as it wen' on, it became more.....'
'More intense, I suppose. Like when ye see them owld pop videos from the Seventies. Ye kna, Slade, Elton John? There's bright blurred colours and the telly's got trailers everywhere. Ye kna? Ye see it even when yer eyes are shut. Supposedly some people can actually see

normally wi' their eyes shut. Even blindfolded.'

'I'd love to gan ower to India. There's a festival there. Cumb Mella. Massive. Gurus wi' their hand in the air for years, people not cutting their hair, or their nails. Deed lang finger nails and toe nails. Saw it on a documentary. Well all this shit's been gannin' on wi' these blokes for years, Man.'

'As I was sayin' though. Ye get an aura, and see all sorts of lights and ye'll see the light o' life. That's where the term 'see the light ' comes from. And that's the light o' heaven. Ye gan through a tunnel and approach a light. Some people have an oot o' body experience. Astral plane, all that. Well people see the light and they're changed. You need to see it Pet. You'll niver look at anything the same way again. Tellin' ye. Life's too short.'

'Why d'ye think the Beatles sang *All Ye Need is Love*? It's cos that's what they were learnin'. Nowt else makes a ha'p'orth o' difference Siobhan. All ye need is love. Take it wherever and whenever ye can, Pet.'

Celia picked up the ashtray from the arm rest and stubbed out the roll-up.

'Fuckin' Hell, man! That was hot. Me throat.'

Siobhan sat up and looked at Celia.

'I've never heard of any of this. Have you seen it then?'

'Aye. They talk aboot the Chakras. Ye see, imagine yer whole body stripped away, All that is left is the spine from yer arse and pelvis. Its called yer coccyx and it gans reet up to yer heed. Just like the model I gave ye. Well the spine is connected to the skull by a bone that moves and lets ye look aroond. That's the atlas. Ever heard of Atlas holdin' up the world? He was a Greek god, I think. Anyway had to take the world on he's shoulders.'

'Yeah Celia. Seen him. He used to be on an ad, I think.'

'Well he's named after the bone. And that leads the spinal chord into the brain by a gland called the pineal gland. That's yer third eye, ye see. And this gland, well it creates hormones to run up and doon the spine in a spiral. Up an' doon. Ye seen the DNA sign. That's the way it gans, roond and doon then back up again.'

'An' the Monarch, after the butterfly. That's the name o' the bone howldin' it in place. Keeps yer brain safe. Most important bone in yer body, like.'

'Anyway, the name of the hormone. Guess what its called? Well its been called the Christos. Aye. Think aboot that.'

'Ye see there's a snake running up and doon yer back, yer spine. That is called Kundalini. When ye have the waves up an doon yer spine, its the Kundalini, the snake from the Garden of Eden teachin' ye the way.'

'Oh, I felt that earlier, I think.'

'Whay aye. Ye did, but that's a bit diff'rent.'

'It's all aboot the Chakras. The Indians, they talk aboot lotus floowers. Well that's cos the Chakras are energy centres. Aye, they look like movin' lotuses – bit like chrysanthemums, ye kna the ones they have at the leek and floower shows. Well there's seven Chakras gannin' up the body. Up yer spine, like. An' you need to get them activated so they start resonatin' in the reet order. That's when the Kundalini, the snake, comes into it.'

'Ye've got the base, the bottom o' yer spine, the fanny (or bollocks for the lads), stomach, yer solar plexus – just there.'

Celia touched her midriff.

'Ye've got yer heart, then the throat. Once all these chakras are activated – and it takes loads o' study an' practising to get it all reet, an' in the reet order. Well as ye gan up the spine you reach the Monarch area. Yer pineal or third eye. That's the key. Once ye get that workin' that's when it all happens. That opens up yer crown chakra. The top o' yer heed. That's when ye can commune wi' all the universe. Commune, that's what they call it. Like communin' wi' God. Though I divn't believe in God. Not the normal way, anyway.'

'Imagine yer spine and yer brain. Think of a picture from school o' the brain. Loads a nerves and blood vessels. Well it looks just like a tree. Doesn't it? Aye. That's the tree o' knowledge in the Garden of Eden and the snake's wrigglin' its way up and doon. Slitherin' and sliding up an' doon an' showing you the way to knowledge. Adam an' Eve, ye see. But it gans back much forther than that, mind. Gans back thoosands o' years to the borth o' man. Or woman, eh? Mebe before.'

'The model o' the spine, I gi' ye. That's the Stairway to Heaven. Ye see it has thorty-three steps. That's a sacred number. An' you climb the thirty-three steps to heaven.'

'Sex is a great way to get it. The Chinese and Indians. Tantric sex. Ganna get into that some time. But imagine looking up yer spine towards the Sun. Its called Jacob's ladder, 'cos the prophet Jacob went up to Heaven. He's in the Bible.'

'Have ye heard of Golgotha? Where Jesus was crucified. Well it means 'place of the skull.' Its the place where the cross was placed. If you look at your body again, you can see how it makes up a cross. There, yer spine and yer shoulders. Christ is hung up on top. Golgotha. Ye see? The Monarch, think of it as the top 'o the cross.'

'Another thing, Heaven. It means to heave up. You kna, tug-o-war. Heave... Well its Christ beein' heaved up. Or us ourselves, even. Raised up. Heaven.'

"Oh Ce. I feel absolutely off me head.'

'Yer a'reet Pet. Just lie doon there.'

Are ye listenin' Siobhan? Can ye hear me?'

'Yeah, Yeah, I am listening. Go on. Very interesting. A lot to take in, though.'

'I'm not religious. I just kna it's just that all the religions, all o' them, deal in steps to heaven until you can literally see the light. Then ye're at peace. At one wi' the universe. And ye divn't have to wait until ye die to find it. Just open the eye. The Monarch'll show ye, like.'

'I'll teach ye.'

'Ye kna'. Some people even get ringin' in their ears, and even holes in their hands. Stigmata, it's called. Like ye've had nails in yer hands like Jesus on the cross. Its fuckin' intense, Man!'

Siobhan looked up.

'There are tales of that happening all over Ireland. Nuns especially.'

'Aye, and ye divn't need drugs either.'

'I'm ganna show ye Pet. Decided that neet in the Toon, remember, when Jerry was in hospit'l. Well I'm takin' ye under me wing. Nae bother Pet.'

'Siobhan. Siobhan! D'ye wanna make another joint? Siobhan! Are ye asleep?'

Chapter 35

The photocopy machine whirred and buzzed, lights flashing repeatedly as it ejected pages into the sorting trays at its side. Colin looked at his watch, and then at Rachael, his colleague. He smiled awkwardly.

'Sorry. Only a few more.'

Rachael looked at him and smiled back politely but without sincerity. Although Colin had only recently joined the department, he was already seen as a favourite in the school, and Rachael saw, through Colin, that her chances of remaining beyond the Summer were now less than prior to his appearance. His accent, though quite understandable Geordie, contrasted with her own RP. Her Buckinghamshire upbringing, private education and fashionable demeanour set her apart from her new colleague, and whilst she was good at her job, and well in with most people in and around the English faculty, Colin seemed to tick all of the new boxes. His local upbringing, especially, was now in keeping with James Fisher, the Principal's, policy of creating a regional hub of learning, and one which promoted working class people in their own areas.

Ironic. She thought of James' Irish twang, its contrast with her own 'proper English' accent, and how she occasionally playfully referred to him as Seamus – Irish for James.

'At last!'

Colin picked out the stapled copies of his dozen booklets,

newly printed and sorted. 'Sorry Rachael.'

Sweating, he rushed away towards his seminar room as Rachael smiled and dismissed his apologies as unnecessary. She knew from experience the difficulties presented by the ageing photocopying machine, and how it often led to queues of lecturers hurrying to try to get to lectures before their students' arrival. Seamus never had that problem, mind.

She placed a pile of A4 onto the lid of the copier and pressed the copy button. It lit, gulped noisily at the pages and began printing into the booklets preset by Colin. She covered her smile with her forearm, watching him trip and pick up his bundled papers.

'Are you OK there, Col?' she shouted down the corridor on recovery of her demeanour. She thought of *Linked In*. Hopefully he'd got back to her.

'How's it going Col?'

'Oh, Hello James. Er, fine. Just heading over to Bedson now. In a bit of a rush, but all sorted.'

'I hear all's well with the class. Very positive. All very good news. Got the results back from Speaking and Listening. Perhaps you'll pop up and see me in my office afterwards, can you?'

'Of course James. See you then.'

'Good.' James passed along the corridor in the direction of the photocopier.

'Hi Seamus. Lovely afternoon.'

'Hi Rachael.'

He smiled at her and laughed along. She was the only one to call him Seamus. She was a great teacher. Knew her stuff. Had the students eating out of her hand. Excellent. If only she liked people a bit more.

'I've been taken by your enthusiasm as well as your ability to teach, Col. We all have. Very interesting approach, and an impressive job you've done.'

Colin sighed inwardly and felt his colour return to normal. His temperature cooled. He could feel his pulse no longer as the pounding in his head began to ease.

'We have been keeping an eye on everything you have been doing, and we are so far most impressed. How do you feel about things? Have you enjoyed your time here so far this Summer?'

Colin smiled at James and nodded.

'I really have had a great time James. It has been the best Summer I can remember.'

Best not to mention the other great Summers. Don't dampen the outward enthusiasm.

'As you know, we are looking to keep on a few of the temporary staff. We always recruit annually like this. The Pre-Sessional is a great way of getting to know people, seeing how they work and if they are suitable candidates to join the faculty.'

Colin uttered an automatic 'Yes,' and another, as he followed along to the words of his boss.

'We have been looking for new blood in particular. We were kind of intrigued over your approach. Very different from nearly everyone else. We thought we would see how you would get on. It's fair to say you and Rachael have very similar teaching styles. Breaths of fresh air.'

Colin again reddened, and felt a slight buzz in his ears, tinnitus ringing, increasing in intensity. It stopped as James smiled and offered him a post on the permanent staff.

'You'll have to begin soon afterwards, mind Col. Very little break. You'll be back next Friday to start all this again. Ear to the ground and shoulder to the grind-stone, eh? We'll need a week to get you allocated to another pair of cohorts and settled in. At least you won't be so pushed for time this coming year though.'

Colin, wishing to punch the air and celebrate like a World Cup goal scorer, smiled politely. Warmly.

'Is that alright? I take it you want the position.'

'Thanks James. I'd love to join permanently.'

'Well done Colin. It will be on a three month probationary period, but I'm certain all will go well.'

Colin stood and grasped the outstretched hand before him and noticed the large gold upturned Claddagh, bigger than the silver one he'd bought Siobhan in Galway. Salt Hill actually.

'If you could make an appointment with Mel. She will go over everything with you: salary; your new contract and such like.'

'See you next week then.'

Chapter 36

www.GraceDarling.co.uk
The Grace Darling Website - Legendary Victorian Heroine.
Welcome to the Grace Darling website
Grace was born on 24th November 1815 at Bamburgh, Northumberland and spent her youth in two lighthouses (Brownsman and Longstone) where her father, William, was the keeper. In the early hours of the 7th September 1838, Grace, looking out from an upstairs window of the Longstone Lighthouse on the Farne Islands, spotted the wreck and survivors of the Forfarshire on Big Harcar, a low rocky outcrop. The Forfarshire had foundered on the rocks and broken in half; one of the halves had sunk during the night. Amidst tempestuous waves and gale force winds there followed an amazing rescue of the survivors.

'That's wrong for a start. Victoria hadn't even been crowned by then. She died in 1838, doesn't it say? Well it couldn't be Victorian until at least 1840, could it? Must have been Regency or Georgian.'
'Aidan looked at his dad, and wondered where he got all the knowledge from.
'Off again,' thought Siobhan.

'Maybe she was a Victorian hero after her death. You know? Didn't become a hero until after 1840. Ever thought of that, smart arse?'

Aidan looked across from his mam to his dad. Expecting a riposte.

'Aye, I suppose,' replied Colin.

Siobhan unbuckled Aidan's seat and lifted him over to her knee on the passenger seat. Should we go to the graveyard, son?'

Aidan looked up at the crags above at the castle perched high on top.

'Look at the fort Mam? Can we go in? Mam? Dad?'

'No son. I think we've had enough of castles for a while.'

Colin opened the door and stepped out onto the car park, and walked over to the pay and display ticket dispenser. He returned with a ticket and placed it face up inside the window. Sixty pence an hour. We'll stay until half two. That should be long enough.'

'Yes,' Siobhan agreed, buckling the red and black straps on the boy's buggy.

'Can I have a biscuit? Please?' he asked, looking up and smiling.

Siobhan offered him a cheese sandwich, which she unwrapped from a crumpled tissue in her pocket. Aidan took it and bit the half eaten soggy bread.

'What a lovely place this is Colin.'

The sun was shining above beyond the castle, and it was warm, even in the shade of the crag above. The three made their way down the road and over towards the church where the heroine was interred, following the sign.

'Look Mam. Seagull.'

A herring gull swooped and lifted the remainder of the

sandwich from the boys hand with its bill, narrowly missing his face with its wings. Before anyone could react, the bird was resting a few metres away, devouring the bread and cheese, staring at the family in case of any sudden movement. Colin rushed over to the grass and shooed, but the bird, after fluttering a few feet, continued to stare at him and Aidan. Siobhan bent down to comfort the frightened lad, and to ensure he wasn't hurt in any way.

'Fucking Hell! They're a proper nuisance now. It could have had his eye out or anything.' Colin walked back to the pair, ignoring the bird and satisfied that it was no longer a threat.'

'Better not give him anything else until we get back in the car,' he said.

'Bird lovers! The RSPB used to cull those around here. But that caused a massive stink. They'd been killing off the gulls to make way for terns and other birds all up the coast. Farne Islands and Coquet Island in particular. *The Observer* got hold o' the story. They stopped it pretty sharpish.'

'Bad bird!' said Aidan.

'Nana had birdie. Green and white. And yellow. Pretty boy. Pretty boy. Billy. Where's Nana? Granddad? Ireland. Ferry to Scouser. Tayto 'n' juice. Sugatea.'

'We used to come here when I was in my late teens.'
Siobhan looked out of the widow at the dunes and marram grass as the car swept onto the causeway. It was unbelievable how flat the rippled sand was. Birdwatching had always been a hobby, and she spent many hours on the Sligo and Donegal coasts as a girl. Waders had always been her favourite – she had always thought of

them as part of a mini safari, and she used to pretend that she was going on an adventure every time she headed to the dunes. No doubt, the coast up here reminded her of home.

Home. Her husband was undoubtedly the love of her life. Those who thought him pompous and self-absorbed, and there were some, she dismissed as narrow minded. Her mother never really got him either.

Colin was certainly one who liked to hear the sound of his own voice, yes, but what could you expect of someone who spends his time speaking, teaching and lecturing. To Siobhan, Colin was a charismatic chatterbox, and she happily drifted in and out of consciousness, happily listening to his incessant twang. She had never heard anyone speak like him when they had met. Six years her junior, he had wooed her easily, or so she'd believed. Only after they were married had Colin told her that he had been obsessed by her the day he'd first spoken with her. She found it endearing, even after they'd wed, that this confident young man had found her approval of such importance. Never had it crossed her mind that his general demeanour, so suited to lecturing, was a cause for concern in their relationship.

Today, Aidan's birthday, was all about the three of them as a family. Luckily, like many couples she had heard of, they never squabbled over naming him. The second scan at six months had settled that the baby was to be a boy. They had easily avoided name discussions henceforth. Perhaps she would hint occasionally and Colin would decline, or nod quietly. Similarly, Colin would offer examples of names he didn't like and contrast them with those he did – They both howled with laughter at the name Royston. Strangely, the name Aidan had arisen, as if from the ether. Both agreed immediately that their little boy would be named after the Irish saint who made his home in Lindisfarne. Colin had always romantically impressed on everyone the name's symbolism of the marriage between Northumbria and Ireland. She went along happily, as usual.

'Its unbelievable that people have to use that, Siobhan, don't you think?'
She stared at the wooden tower outside.
'Let's take a look, should we? Maybe we can spend the night in it.'
'Fuck off, will you? Before we do get stuck here.'
Colin restarted the car and they drove over to the island, leaving the beehive like structure behind.
Siobhan had every reason to celebrate. As a Catholic, she often felt alone in her faith. Colin never interfered in her thoughts, and he had begun his courtship by eulogising the benefits of faith. Unlike every man she had met, not many were willing to give her this unquestioned acceptance. Colin, a confirmed existentialist, had said he had sometimes wished he wasn't an atheist. Faith, if believable, would be a great comfort. But it wasn't for him. They had both accepted this, and there wasn't much else to be said. Until Aidan had come along anyway.
Colin had not really got behind her attempts to bring the boy up in the Catholic faith. Oh, he hadn't prohibited anything, or complained in any way. Just let him try, she thought. But he just didn't get the importance of it all. But at least he was happy to let her bring him up as she thought fit in this respect.
Just before they headed North, though, just before this trip, Colin had confided that he wished to have Aidan

blessed in St Aidan's Church on the island. The trip to Lindisfarne, he said, would be where they would further cement their love for Aidan and each other. A special self-baptism on top of that they'd undertaken back in Ireland four years earlier. Colin had affirmed that, as an atheist, and having been brought up that way by his dad from a young age, spirituality had been sadly lacking. Colin didn't want that void for Aidan. Give him a choice. This would put the icing on the cake and ensure everyone was invested. Siobhan had kissed him lovingly when he uttered these words. So much for egotism, she thought. No one knew him like she did – and she loved him all the more.

'I'm surprised how modern this place is Siobhan.'
'You'd think it was a bit older, wouldn't you?'
The church looked more mundane than both had imagined. They both pushed the door to the pink porch and entered the wooden shed-like structure. Inside, although more like the church one would expect, a white room flooded with light from several windows and the aisle laid with red carpeting, there was no doubt this church was a lot more Spartan than they had expected.
Siobhan looked over the Stations of the Cross, all of which were sculpted from light brown wood. As a Catholic, she had never seen wooden sculpted imagery thus in an English church, and this made the church seem ever more real to her.
Colin looked around and was impressed by the simplicity of the interior. The outside reminded him of a Pentecostal church, and he was not prepared for the beautiful symmetrical simplicity he was now viewing. The Stations of the Cross were the only obvious indications that he

was standing in a Catholic Church, and he thought this better than that he had had the boy baptised in.

'This is just like the church I was Christened in Siobhan. Never have thought it was Catholic. Then I suppose they were all Catholic in the old days.'

Siobhan ignored him. His stating of the obvious seemed like more idle chatter. She wanted to cherish this moment.

'Hello. Hello. Aye, it's Bill. What's up?'

'Hang on a minute. I cannit hear ye. Hang on. Can you hear me? There. That better?'

Bill raced back and forth around the lobby, seemingly oblivious to the receptionist and the couple sat in the sofa to his left. Increasingly agitated, his voice rose and fell, growling and whispering in turn. The odd barked obscenity punctuated the calm atmosphere to the annoyance of the couple.

'Excuse me Pal. Can you rein it in?'

'Oh! Sorry.' Bill, his hand over the mobile phone mic, looked over briefly at the man before smiling in apology.

'Bill. Can you please calm down?'

He turned and looked over the phone towards the young woman behind the reception desk.

'I'm sorry Pet.'

'Hang on Frank. I'll ring you back. Just give us a minute. I'll gan upstairs.'

Bill retreated from the lobby and turned around the corner before pressing the lift button. Tense, he waited. A moment later the lift bell pinged and the doors opened, a small linoleum lined closet awaited, and Arthur strode in. Turning to face the closing doors, he reached out and pressed the illuminated top button. The elevator began its ascent, the room shook and trembled until it suddenly stopped with a jerk. The doors parted from the middle.

A short balding figure stood in front of the lift. His top coat open, he reached in and pulled out an envelope.

'Bill Jewers, you've been served. Siobhan Compton says 'Hello.''

The envelope, flicked from the man's hand and hurtled into the lift, hitting Arthur on the shoulder before dropping onto the lino.

'Aidan. Come on Son. Come here. Look at the font.'

What's a font?

'Its a little bath, but its special. Come here.'

'Come on Colin!'

He stood behind the lectern, about to deliver a mock lecture.

'Stop it Colin, not here. Not now.'

Colin joined them at the table beside the font.

Aidan joined the pair at the little recess, inset into the wall, near the door.

'Righto. Lets do this,' said Colin.

'What the fuck's this? What d'ye mean?'

Dan held the phone close to his face and bellowed at Davy on the other end.

'I don't give a fuck what she says. I'm not selling. I'm telling ye? Its bollocks. Load 'o shite. Who does she think she is? Who d'ye think ye are?'

The phone receiver shattered onto the floor, shards scattering along the tiled floor. Robson walked back towards the spa and reread the words on the paper he carried. The Monarch logo, newly created, glared up at him from the top. The crowned butterfly.

'Pretentious shite,' he said as he read.

LETTER BEFORE ACTION

True, Jerry Compton did lend him a fair amount, and it was agreed that he could pay it back as and when, an' all. Why was she calling it in? Now? He had to think. Think of a new plan. Sure, he'd seen this coming. The last time he met her and Davy they'd said they wanted the money or they'd be calling it in. But he never thought they'd go this far. What could he do?

He opened the glass smoked door and entered the steam room. Alone, he pondered further on the whys and wherefores of the situation. He could probably put his hands on some of the money, half at a push. He had made this clear to them when they met. Well he hadn't said he could get half. Fuck them! Need to know basis. He knew he was in trouble.

He'd built up the Hexham business from scratch. No one could deny it. Alright, Jerry Compton had provided him with some financial aid. At the beginning. But he hadn't done him any favours. Not really. He took a fair share in interest on the loan, and Dan had hardly missed a payment in the twelve and a half years. In fact he was probably only behind by less than twenty grand. Much less. And that could be made up. They needed to know that he was no push over. The bitch!

He'd already tried that though, hadn't he?

That prick Richie. He should never have let him come. Been a nightmare from the start. Just couldn't keep he's hands to himself. That lass behind the bar. Just couldn't stop himself. Then there was that other one. She had to be sacked. Aye, he had been a prick, a headache, from the beginnin'. He'd deserved that slap. Definitely. Then again, he wasn't a bad kid. He had straightened his-sel' oot, and he was tryin'. He wasn't the reason behind this. Still. Dan felt he should never have agreed to take him on. Look where it had got him.

Sat on the bench, sweating and red, he looked down again and reread the contents of the letter in his hand.

LETTER BEFORE ACTION

He knew this meant business. But how could he resolve it? They had made it clear that they weren't acceptin' a payment, even if it brought the account up to date. The butterfly logo again seemed to mock him. He screwed up the paper and threw it on the tiled floor.

'Bastards!' he shouted. The words were absorbed by the pine walls. He repeated them. Little comfort, but better than nowt.

The orange lit sauna, a hit with the residents, had been the focal point of many a crisis, and it was here that Dan had resolved many of the serious issues his business had faced in the past, not just the arrears owed to Compton. He thought again of the issues with the lad, his protege. Again he thought how the young'un had turned himself around, but to no avail. Surely, that should have allowed him some scope for her to give him time. But no. Not that bitch. And Davy. What a prick. Lost his balls.

He felt the heat. Time to take the plunge. He opened the glass door, this time to alight and stepped out into the spa area. He got the bucket and filled it. Cold water drenched him as he upturned the wooden bucket above him. He re-entered the sauna. Ninety-two degrees. He bent and picked the wooden spoon from the water bucket and doused the stones. Accompanying the hiss, the heat burned and he retreated to the corner of the sauna. He settled on the bottom bench. Never could understand how people could manage to sit on the higher seats. Unbearable!

The logo stared up at him, the letter before action unfurling on the pine floor, soggy, ink running in the steaming heat. The blurred butterfly nevertheless threatened ruin, and he knew it. It was hot. He never had got fully comfortable with the heat, but knew it was good for him. For his blood pressure. Didn't know about the cholesterol, mind. But it couldn't do any harm, surely.

He thought of the sauna, and how he seemed the only one to use it nowadays. Perhaps they've got a point, after all. Increasingly, he was the sole user of the spa. Crowded, or at least used regularly, by guests only a couple of years ago, he now seemed the only one using it. Ever. He even tried opening it up to the locals. A fiver a go. But hardly anyone had come. Half a dozen, maybe. Maybe.

But it was great, especially as a place to hide away and think. To think over his problems.

The bar, that had been a real winner, though. Even when people weren't staying, as was increasingly the case over the last couple of years. At least the takings were healthy there. The County, Hexham's best hostelry, never disappointed as a watering hole. He thought of the nights, especially on weekends, when the place had hummed with people. Dancing and singing in the function room, which he had hired out pretty regularly, at least enough to almost cover its costs. The jukebox, which he hadn't had to subsidise much, was frequently playing in the bar and lounge, although, he admitted, not as often as at the beginning.

He thought of the fight with young Compton again. He

hadn't put up a fight. And he could take a beatin'. He just punched him a couple of times, once in the solar plexus, and then on the chin. A swift uppercut. Beauty. The lad had bent down after the blow to his stomach, almost like he was eager to meet his right hand. Spark oot. Rich had lay doon on the carpet. Hadn't woke up for a good few seconds. More than the count to ten, anyway. Scared him at first, but he'd deserved it. The barmaid ran oot screamin' Never saw the little minx again.

'Ye see,' I said after. 'Not worth it.'

Rich had agreed then. Been a good lad, mostly, ever since. Just needed a lesson, that was all.

What a fuckin' cheek. What did she expect? Think I'm ganna let Jerry Compton's laddie take the piss? When I'm daeing him a favour? Some people!

The butterfly logo, atop the discarded letter, sodden and almost completely unfurled, its black outline running across the page in splodges, looked at him. He rose up and lunged over, aiming his bare right foot in a kick. As it missed, as it flew almost a foot above, the mis-timed kick followed through and glanced off the pine bench in beside the smoked glass door. He howled in agony, and his left foot hopped over in the direction of the logo. He hopped, placed both hands horizontal in an attempt to regain his balance. The floor, slippery with condensed steam, repelled him and he was unable to gain purchase. More like a rink now, he scrabbled for anything to gain control, and his right hand arced to grab the rail enclosing the stove. He grabbed and his hand burned, searing on the grey granite. He moved his left hand but it was too late. Falling, Dan seemed to butt the rail, his eye catching directly onto the corner of the stove rail, the edge of its wooden frame pushing into his socket. He screamed as he fell. His head rebounded off the floor. He groaned. Again he groaned, then passed out on the sodden floor.

The Monarch logo lay next to him, its outline sodden and blotted. Its crown running into the butterfly's head below.

Siobhan lifted Aidan, who smiled as she took him closer for a look at the water inside.

Colin wet his hand in the font, then marked the sign of a cross on the boy's forehead.

'Ugh! Dad!' Aidan turned up his nose and turned to cuddle into his mother's neck.

'There you are Son,' said Colin. 'Anointed Aidan in St Aidan's Church, Lindisfarne. Something to tell the girls when you're older.'

Siobhan laughed along – Colin always laughed at his own jokes. For comic effect? Probably to let people know he was joking.

Colin looked around for a sign on the road.

'Better make sure we don't get a ticket.'

'What? You're not gonna get one here,' said Siobhan.

'I don't know. Remember that time outside the British Museum?'

'How could I forget?' thought Siobhan.

'I mean, I couldn't believe that. Parking charges just for parking outside someone's house. Camden Council. Fucking disgrace! It's like someone parking outside my house and having to pay.'

Siobhan knew this and switched off again before pointing out the sign.

'See. No charges.'

They moved on to the visitor centre, Siobhan and Aidan holding hands. Colin running to catch up, corduroy jacket hanging awkwardly over one shoulder as he attempted to jump into the other sleeve.

'Here. There's one here for you George. Here.'
Geordie picked the letter off the quilt, ruffled and stained from the night's activities. Awoken late, Avril went to the doorway and took the bundle of letters from the welcome mat. He needs to stop usin' this address.
'You need to stop putting yersel' doon as livin' here George. If the landlord finds oot.'
'Who Frank? Just leave Frank to me. He's a good mate. I'll talk him roond. If he ever finds oot, mind.'
'Just stop George, will ye?'
'Just shut the fuck up moanin'. Moanin' all the time!'
'George!'
'I said shut it Avril, or I'll borst ye. I mean it.'
Avril retreated into the kitchen and muttered protestations. What did she see in George Collins anyway? She opened the kettle lid and placed it beneath the rubber spout of the tap.
'What the fuck is this? What?'
Looking around Avril glanced at George. Geordie Collins. Big hard man. Well she knew better, didn't she. She suppressed a laugh as she watched her boyfriend cringe as he looked at the letter in his hand.
'Whoa, Avril. What does this mean? D'ye kna this word? And this? Come here!'
Avril placed the kettle on the gas hob, and tiptoed barefooted into the studio room. Light shone through the sash window, diffuse brilliance through filtering white nets, framed by red velvet curtains and hanging pelmet. She took the paper from Geordie. Quality beige bond paper folded neatly into three sections. A crowned

butterfly, wings outstretched amid the upper section atop the words 'The Monarch.' Below, in upper case, the words:

LETTER BEFORE ACTION

'Look Mam. Look at this.'
Siobhan strode over to where Aidan stood.
'Its a snake, said Aidan.'
Probably symbolising evil.
'The devil and the garden of Eden,' said Colin, absently, as he fumbled with his keys.
'Lift me up Dad, I want to see.'
As he did so Siobhan read the imprint next to the illumination. She thought of the page she'd read earlier on the way to the island:

> The *Lindisfarne Gospels* are presumed to be the work of a monk named Eadfrith, who became Bishop of Lindisfarne in 698 and died in 721. Current scholarship indicates a date around 715, and it is believed they were produced in honour of St. Cuthbert. However, some parts of the manuscript were left unfinished so it is likely that Eadfrith was still working on it at his time of death. It is also possible that he produced them prior to 698, in order to commemorate the elevation of Cuthbert's relics in that year, which is also thought to have been the occasion for which the St Cuthbert Gospel (also British Library) was produced. The Gospels are richly illustrated in the insular

style and were originally encased in a fine leather treasure binding covered with jewels and metals made by Billfrith the Anchorite in the 8th century. During the Viking raids on Lindisfarne this jewelled cover was lost and a replacement was made in 1852. The text is written in insular script, and is the best documented and most complete insular manuscript of the period.

She looked at the facsimile in front of her and thought back to the day in Dublin as a child.

'This Guinness is like mother's milk.'
Dad was sat next to the server on a large table, his back to the wall on a red velvet settle opposite his wife and daughter.
'I've been coming here since I was a teenager. Best bar in Dublin!'
Her mother was not impressed and knew that Damien was only just getting warmed up.
As another customer walked away with a steaming plate of stew, she dropped a fork on the floor. 'Fuckin' bastard!' She hurried on and disappeared out of sight.
'What a fucker!' said Dad.
'Shush, will ya?' added Siobhan's mother. This could be another prelude to trouble, she feared.
'Get yoursel' another.' Damien laughed, addressing the woman on her return to the food counter. She smiled in return to Damien's friendly grin.
Siobhan smiled along, relieved that the woman seemed friendly.
'Where ya from, like? Just down for the day? The

woman's enquiry was welcomed warmly, and Siobhan's mother smiled, adding that they were off to see the *Book of Kells*.

'Aw, they're fabulous. Gorgeous,' replied the woman. 'Where are you from then?'

'Carrick-on-Shannon We just came down on the train.'

'Should ha' brought the car. Cost a fortune. Feckin' rip-off!'

Damien drained the black stuff and looked at the froth gathered down the inside of the glass. Light golden ringlets above a slimy liquid.

'Look at that! Never get that in England. Would you like a drink my love? I'm just going over to the bar.'

The woman looked him up and down, looked at his family sitting there, and replied.

'Thanks a million, but I've got me dinner over there, and I'm off back soon. Have a lovely day.'

She picked up a knife and fork from the grey tray on the stainless steel table, smiled and headed back around to the other side of the L-shaped room, which was busier.

'Can we not sit round there Ma?' asked Siobhan.

'No. Kids aren't allowed round there. And this isn't the place for kids, anyway.'

'Conway's is the place for everyone,' replied her husband through gritted teeth.' He opened his mouth and dropped two packets of Tayto and a bag of peanuts onto the rectangular beer stained table, placing three full glasses beside them.

'This place is so filthy Damien. Look at the carpet. For God's sake!'

'You shouldn't take the Lord's name in vain. It's not right,' he mocked. 'And that shows this is a quality place – plenty people drinking. Not plum-arsin' around sniffing

and rabbitin' about the drink. Real people in a real bar!'
'In some of the bars in London you'll do well to get a pint at all. Poncey wine bars everywhere. All they do is rabbit.'
Siobhan looked puzzled.
'That means talk. Cockney. Rabbit and Pork. Talk. Chas and Dave.'
'England. Why would you want to go there anyway?' thought Siobhan.

'No son, It's not a snake, its just a letter.'
'It is a snake. It is. Isn't it Mam?'
'Aidan, it looks a bit like a snake.'
'Aye, but it isn't. It's an illuminated manuscript.'
They all looked at the page in front of them, on display in the glass case, four spotlights coiled around like four heads of serpents shedding their light on the facsimile inside.
'It's not the actual book. That's in the British Library,' said Colin. 'Caused a stink round here when they took it down South. It's supposed to stay in Durham Cathedral. Should be here though.'
'The *Book of Kells* is kept in Dublin. Just the same. Suppose more people can see it in the capital.'
'What's the *Book of Kells* got to do with it?' challenged Colin.
'Well, if you look at this page it looks very like the one in Kells. Almost identical. You see, this is the title page of the Gospel of Matthew. See the snakes you are looking at aren't snakes at all. They are letters.'

Liber Generationis.

'You see. The three snakes heads are the beginning *L I B*.

Siobhan thought of the page she had seen all those years ago in Trinity. It really was amazing that she was looking at the same pages all these miles, and years, apart. But there was no mistaking it. These were the same pages. OK, a little different. This one did seem to portray snakes. With eyes and heads pointing upward. The Kells version was the same though, although that was surrounded by people. Crudely portrayed, yes. But finely coloured. And there was no doubt, whatever Aidan thought, they were looking at the letters *L I B*, just as in Kells.

'Maybe they are trying to allude to Adam and Eve. You know the serpent and the Garden of Eden,' added Colin.

'No!' affirmed Siobhan. 'I know the picture. In Dublin its the same. *L I B*. Look its all part of the text.'

L,I, B, e,r

'See? And then it says 'G, e,n,e,r,a, t,''

'Yes. I know. I can see that. Looks more like a C, mind.'

Liber Cenerat...

'Not sure about the rest.'

'Always wondered why everyone seemed to be obsessed with snakes in those days. Seems to be an important theme throughout history. Did you know that the UN logo has a snake in the middle? Coiled round a staff on top of a map of the world. Or is it the World Health Organisation? Same thing really. Always wondered.'

'Let's go!' said Siobhan, and picked up the child before heading back to the entrance. 'Off again!' she thought.

Armstrong walked up the cobbled road on his way to The Globe. With Jerry out the way, everything should have been a doddle. No way should he be facing ruin, as he was now.

Mary had handed him the envelope and he had opened it carelessly. At the height of his success, and basking in the knowledge that all his plans, a large majority of them anyway, were coming to fruition, he had not expected the letter from Siobhan. The little bitch!

Ahead he looked at the sign hanging above the half bay window. He approached and thought of whisky. Just a quick one in the Dirty Bottles, and he'd still have plenty of time to make it in time. The flags, planed smooth from years of rain and footprints, stretched ahead, as a kind of route to salvation. Aye. Just the one.

He hurried up the hill and approached the bay on Narrowgate. He stopped beneath the sign, unusual in his curiosity. He had countlessly passed this spot, entered, exited and glanced into the bay. Today, things seemed different.

The butterfly, atop the letter, crowned above, titled below:

The Monarch

Never heard of it. He read on.

LETTER BEFORE ACTION

Siobhan Compton, Proprietor. She'd got her feet under that table pretty quick. Not even a year since I'd met the little twat. And now she's telling me how to gan on.

I'll give her a good scuddin' when I see 'er. Won't kna

what's hit her. Fuckin' cheek!

He paused and looked in. Really looked in, this time. For a change.

He looked up toward the eaves. Stepped back and surveyed the white stuccoed wall and looked down again.

The Dirty Bottles

The plaque above the bay, fringed in badly nailed lead, paint cracking through years of weathering, indicated a fitting image for today.

Needs a proper clean up. Not just the bottles that are dorty.

He stepped forward again and looked through the Georgian Bay. Dickensian Gothic, the bottles lay scattered and strewn among cobwebs and dust. Two upright, the rest on their sides amongst rotting wooden crates. Left there by the last publican to move them. Dropped as he moved these cursed empties. Relics of the pub's Victorian past, its legacy to today's tourists, and the conmen in the brewery.

'Bollocks. Get that little bitch to move them.'

He laughed. He moved his wrist revealing his Rolex. Its Oyster clasp twisted and revealed its gold face and black numerals. Half past IIII. Plenty o' time.

The second hand twitched repeatedly on its way around the dial. He focused on the timepiece, framed on the left by his striped cuff. The crown, the trademark, seldom seen on the bezel, as was this one, put this watch into the better category. A different league. Plenty of people would be wanting to buy them, he knew. Best fakes in the North East. Who'd kna?

The gloom above the bottles, through the window and

above the display frame, now seemed uninviting. Even whisky, knock-down priced as it was, couldn't tempt him now. He turned, looked at the cobbles ahead leading onto Fenkle Street. The Olde Cross could wait and he ambled onward. Upward as he approached the square ahead.

Oncoming, a Mondeo approached. Looking across, up across the road, Armstrong paused. An ox-blood brogue shone below, above the kerb. He lifted it in readiness to step forth after the car's departure. He held it steadily, the newly polished immaculate shoe hanging in the air, topped by the slightly frayed Argyle check, burgundy and grey.

'I need new socks.'

The car passed and he stepped forward. The sole, polished smooth with use, unable to grip the granite below, slipped, glancing off the slippery cobble. Frank, sensing his fall, placed his hand before him. His strength, less than it used to be, couldn't hold his weight this time, such was the recent weight gain. He fell. Full force taken by his hands, the heels scuffed and knees stung. His mouth battered a cobble and rebounded. His lip, forced onto the bottom of his top incisor, was pierced. Blood dripped. His tooth dropped onto the ground settling in the crack between two cobble stones.

'Yer alreet Mate! Yer alreet! Let us help you. Mebe stay there.'

The young man bent down and placed his hand on the old man's shoulder. Blood flowed onto the stones and he placed Frank's white handkerchief on his opened forehead to stem the blood dripping from his eyebrow. Their shadow reached further and further down the gold glazed road as Frank was motioned to the side of the street.

'Do you want some mead, Siobhan?' Asked Colin.

'That's that sickly honey wine the monks used to drink, isn't it?' she asked, looking at the Old English lettering on the outside wall.

'I want some mead, I want some mead,' sung the boy.

'Forget it,' said Siobhan.

They headed over towards the car.

Chapter 37

'Mon – arch.'

Aidan pushed the door after peering into the restaurant above the white door frame and through the window.

'Mon- Ark. It's pronounced Mon – Ark, Aidan. Its a type of butterfly.'

'Its also a king, Son.'

'Or Queen teased Siobhan.'

She kissed Colin, pulled him into her and held his embrace. Aidan let go of the door and it began to close before the couple. Siobhan pulled away and caught the door just before it closed fully, pushed and stepped inside.

Aidan scampered over to the counter.

'Hiya Son,' said Gillian. 'Siobhan, we had a phone call from Davy earlier. Said to tell ye he towld Arthur. Said we'll not be hearin' from him again. That mean anything to you? He said you'd understand.'

'Oh alright Gill. Thanks for that. I understand. I'll give Davy a ring later.'

Gillian looked down at the boy as he blinked and smiled.

'Do you like the painting?'

Aidan looked at the framed canvas print high above him, behind the bar. The bottom was obscured, but he could see the majority of it. Vivid colourful men sat in a darkened room, three windows the only source of light. Clearly some kind of dinner.

Aidan looked into the paining, or the upper part

discernable to him from beneath the bar, and saw the collection of men ordered around Jesus in the centre.

'Look Mam. Virgin Mary.'

Colin patted the boy's head and laughed at him, looking at Gillian. Colin, the skilled lecturer, now confirmed as such in his new permanent post, proceeded to show off. He played to his audience and motioned to a couple sitting in the window. He turned and addressed the room over his son's head, across the newly fitted oak floor. Repeatedly motioning to the picture as if delivering a PowerPoint he talked and six diners listened as he lectured, his voice audible and assured as he explained the painting's content.

'That is not the Virgin Mary. It's St John. Looks like a girl, mind. It actually led to various conspiracy theories saying Da Vinci included Mary Magdalen into his *Last Supper*.'

'But no. They're the twelve Apostles surrounding Jesus at the Last Supper. He is announcing his coming crucifixion and telling them that each will soon denounce him. The dozen various figures, ordered into four groups of three around the central figure of Jesus.'

Aidan looked up from beneath his father's arm, the painting framed beneath the arc of his armpit.

Colin swept his arm repeatedly around and in front of the picture. He surveyed the scene and pointed out the three windows behind centre, the biggest clearly illuminating the central figure of Jesus. Illuminating his halo from behind so Christ's divine light shone out onto the viewer.

'You note the three windows,' he boomed to the diners. 'It is no coincidence that three windows are there to light the supper. They represent the trinity of the Father, the Son and the Holy Spirit.'

He'd held the attention of two of the diners until the end, and finished his speech.

'Don't get me wrong, mind. Not a religious bone in my body.'

He laughed loudly, but restrained an urge to bow.

Still looking up into the painting, from left to right Aidan saw three men looking at Jesus, one pointing. The next group, the third figure, he knew, was a lady next to Jesus. She looked away as her group talked amongst themselves.

'Look at the back of the picture, Mam. The room's nearly bare.'

The background was indeed almost cartoon-like. Unfinished almost, in contrast to the colours radiating towards the central halo of Jesus. The Halo, in contrast to that of the other figures in the picture glared.

Colin turned from his audience and stepped closer to the bar.

'I'll have a glass o' red, please Gill. Siobhan, what you havin'? Are you drivin'? Aidan. What d'ye want to drink son?'

'It's OK Gill. I'll go down and change it. What is it Becks?'

'Aye. Its just gone.'

'I'll be straight back Col. See you in a minute.'

Siobhan took the keys to the cooler from Gill, turned and walked over to the spiral staircase. She unhooked the chain then looked around at her family.

'Aidan, d'ye want to come and have a look in the cellar, Son? Come on.'

Aidan loosened his grip from his dad's hand and followed his mother over to the staircase.'

'I like the way you've decorated the stairs, mind Gill.'
'That was Celia Col. She took charge of everything there. Definitely her baby. Should o' seen it last month. Thought it was scrap. Really came oot good though.'
He and Gill stared at the newly refurbished feature. Celia indeed had transformed the rusting rickety structure, once almost falling apart, so that it now helped light up the bar area and the mezzanine above. The rusted metal was now painted and, woven beneath each of the wrought iron patterned steps, diffused lights emitted an aura as the structure rose up through the restaurant areas and into the spaces directly below. Soft lighting was punctuated intermittently by the slow regular movement of bulbs, flashing in a pattern to give the impression that light was moving up and down the curling banister on either side of the steps. It was obviously descending into the cellar that the lighting feature then ascended from the cellar floor to the newly refurbished office in the attic above at the top of the mezzanine. The lighting traced each of the bannisters alternately up and down.
'Well, Gill. I have to say that Celia has done a great job, then. Good on her. Where is she? I'll tell her me-self.'
Col looked back to the painting and across the bar.
'The place is lookin' great. Well done.'
'I'll have another Prosecco to celebrate, can I?' In fact, make it a Bellini. D'ye know what that is?'
Celia, dressed in a white blouse and black pencil skirt, appeared from the restaurant area behind the bar.
'I'll pop doonstairs Gill. I need to get some Champaign. A'reet Col? How are ye?'
'Never Better Ce, replied Col
'Well done Celia. Very impressive. Looks like Siobhan was right about you two.'

She headed over the floor and descended into the cellar below.

'Hiya Son.' Celia addressed Aidan as she hurried down the stairs into the cellar.

Aidan looked up and watched as Celia's black shoes came down the stairs and into view followed by the rest of her

'Are ye here wi' yer mam Son?

'Mam's in there Celia.' He pointed to the cooler behind.

'Oh Fuck this Celia! What do I do with this thing? Cannot get it to gas up properly.

Celia stepped over to the barrel and unhooked it before reattaching the screw-fit.

'Nae gas Pet. I'll ha'e to change it.'

As she bent over the barrel she saw Siobhan was less than pleased and asked her the reason, a little worried that she may be the cause.

'Oh, I dunno Ce. Just, Col is actin' like a bit of a dick. Ye should have heard him before.'

'What, d'ye mean the lecture?'

'Yeah, Leonardo Da Vinci's *Last Supper*. Just what the customers wanna hear when they're havin' their dinner.'

'Oh, I don't know Siobhan. Quite funny really. He means well. Quite cute really.'

'I think this new job might be going to his head, ye know? Although he's been pretty stressed out with it. Flat out all Summer.'

Celia stood up and walked over to the gas bottle and placed the spanner around the affixing nut, twisting it off.

'I heard him from behind the bar. Shame he can ownly see the obvious.'

'What d'ye mean Celia?'

'Oh, howay Siobhan. He's a great guy, an' all. Loads a qualifications. He's canny, but howay.'

'Celia?'

'I heard him gannin' on aboot the picture. Cannit see the wood for the trees Man.'

Celia pointed to the boxes in the cage in the corner.

'Here's the keys Siobhan. Can ye git a couple o' bottles o' Champaign oot o' the cage there please?'

She switched over the pipe to affix the other gas bottle, tightening the nut before turning on the CO_2

'Ye'd think wi' all that education he'd be able to see the bigger picture.'

'Da Vinci?'

'Hello! Siobhan.'

Siobhan stared from the cage. Grabbing two bottles of Champagne, she looked at her friend and stifled a naughty laugh, sharing the forbidden joke at her husband's expense. Aidan stared, his face illuminated by the intermittently flashing lights as they ascended and descended into the cellar. He began to ascend.

'Listen Siobhan. Da Vinci was a thorty-thord degree Freemason. That's as high as it gans. Thirty three. Steps to heaven. Jacob's Ladder. Remember? Had access to all the books in the Pope's lib'ry. He knew all aoot it. Genius, they say. Properly enlightened.'

'Yeah. Celia, I am glad you chose the picture. You've done a great job with all the cleaning up and decorating. All the renovatin'. It's not been easy. I couldn't be happier. You've really made the place what it is. I knew you were the one to help me here. Thanks.'

'Siobhan. *The Last Supper*. Hello!'

'Its like I said aboot the universe. The Zodiac. Remember. Never mind what Col's on aboot. Can ye not see?'

'See what Ce?'

'Ye've got Jesus in the middle. He's lirr-up cos he's the

Sun, 'e's got twelve roond 'im. They're the Zodiac revolvin' roond the Sun. There's thorteen figures in all, an' there's also a wife there. She's Vorgo. Virgo, ye kna? She's Mary Magdalene.'
'What Ce? Really?'
'Aye. I read aboot it in me book. Listen. Mary means High Priestess. Magdalene, it means Tower o' knowledge. And Jesus – he's Zeus, the chief God. The Sun. That's the Trinity the Chorch gans on aboot all the time. Ye kna? Father, Son an' Holy Ghost.'
'That's interesting Ce. Maybe.'
Siobhan closed the cage and secured the padlock.
'Let's get back, eh?'
'Wait Pet. Ye see, Da Vinci, he's showin' we the connection wi' God through the paintin'. An' ye've got the man, positive, and the lass, negative. Blue – female, red, male. Have a look, ye'll see the two, Jesus and Mary, Vorgo, they're both mirror-rin' each other's colours. Like Harlequin. Ying an' Yang. An' ye can see how 'e's divided all the disciples into four different categ'ries. The differint types o' Zodiac signs all broke up facin' into their little groups, wi' the Sun in the centre. It's all symbolic o' the big picture o' the universe, ye see.'
'I suppose.' Siobhan ascended and peeped over to look at the picture. 'Yeah, I can see that. It makes sense. Kind of.'
'Aidan! Aidan! Get down. Down!'
Ignoring the startled stares from everyone in the room, Siobhan glared up the spiral at Aidan. Stood just below the trap door, he was pushing it. Trying to gain entry to the attic room above.'
'Oh, he's a'reet Siobhan. Let him gan up. Here take the key. Here. I wanted to surprise ye later. But gan up noo. Go on, have a look.'

Siobhan rushed up the staircase and grabbed him to herself.

'Here Son. You'll need this. Open the lock with this.'

Aidan took the key from Siobhan and turned to insert the key in the lock in the ceiling above him.

'I'll switch the light on Pet,' shouted Celia.

Siobhan and Aidan pushed the trap-door which opened upwards into the room.

Siobhan picked him up and carried her son upwards into the light above.

Printed in Great Britain
by Amazon